COYOTE WILD

COYOTE HUNGER BOOK 2

RHIAN CAHILL

Coyote wild
Coyote Hunger Book 2
By Rhian Cahill

For those of you who love the coyotes as much as I do.
For Shannon for taking a chance on the first book and keeping
her head up when life threw a curve ball.
For Grace, because I find your enthusiasm inspiring and your
support unconditional.
For Mari and Nic because without you girls I wouldn't be
where I am in this crazy business.
And, as always, for the boy who promised me the world and the
man who gave it to me. I love you, Babe. Together Forever.

1

NEED SLAMMED into Brogan Wilder like a two-by-four to the gut. He knew lust, dealt with it when it rose, but this...

This was unlike anything he'd ever experienced. The beast inside chafed at the chains of restraint, snarled and snapped to be let free.

Brogan searched the room but nothing he could see should have him ready to shift. His sister Rowan sat on the sofa, his best friend and her fiancé, Quinn, beside her. They were the only others in the room. The fine hairs on the back of his neck stood at attention and the blood in his veins heated and pumped harder. Whatever had his instincts screaming to take, to possess, had moved closer.

Skin grew tight and hot as he fought with his inner beast. Shifting wasn't an option. Not yet. First he needed all his human skills to determine what had the power to do this to him. Then he'd have to decide if it was friend or foe. He sniffed the air, tried to place the feminine scent teasing his senses. It wasn't Rowan or any other female he knew.

"For pity's sake, Brogan, sit down. You're making *me*

nervous and I know you're all bark and no bite. If you don't relax you'll scare El right back to Australia." Rowan's words broke into his agitated thoughts.

"What?" He tried to focus on his sister and what she was saying.

"Eloise. Remember? She'll be coming down from her room any minute and I want you to be on your best behavior. It took months of nagging and pleading to get her to agree to come out for the wedding. I want her to enjoy herself and not regret saying yes."

Rowan pushed off the lounge and came to stand beside him. Placing her hand on his arm she said, "Please, Brogan. She's the best friend I've had since Gordie, the only friend. She likes *me*. Not Brogan's sister."

Brogan looked at her. She was all grown up, ready to face her destiny but not without scars. They all had them but Rowan would have more if it wasn't for Eloise Crawford. He knew their friendship had been what kept his sister from going mad the few years she'd been forced to live away from home. He sucked in a deep breath and let it out slowly.

"Okay, I'll try. But something's got the beast's hackles up and I can't figure out what." He'd never hidden any of the ugly side of who or what he was from Rowan and he wouldn't do it now.

"Rowan?"

A musical voice with a strange sultry accent came at the instant his beast went on red alert and yanked at Brogan's control.

He couldn't keep the growl inside, or stop the change in his eyes that Rowan wouldn't miss. If Brogan's instincts were right, his mate had just stepped into the room.

Rowan's eyes went wide and her face drained of color. Shaking her head, she whispered, "No. Brogan, no."

Brogan squeezed his eyes shut, dragged the beast back under control. It wouldn't do to scare Eloise before they'd even met. When he opened his eyes again it was to find Rowan watching him warily. A rush of breath left her when she saw he had command of his coyote.

"It's not my choice, Rowan. The fates have spoken." He tried to ease her with a hug. Drawing her close he murmured, "You'll need to help guide her."

"No."

"Yes, Rowan. Remember, what's done is done, we move on from here."

She pulled from his arms and stood with hands on hips. "You hurt her and I'll tear you to pieces," she snarled.

Brogan smiled. He had no doubt she'd follow through on her threat. He'd seen her go to battle for someone she cared about. Her loyalty to those she loved was unquestionable, but if those she loved were pitted against each other she always sided with the weaker one.

Rowan looked past him to the woman who stood twenty feet away and had his body reacting as if she were plastered to his side. He could smell her, almost taste her. If he didn't get a hold of himself he had no doubt Eloise Crawford would run screaming into the hills or to the nearest airport and first plane out of there.

"El, you've unpacked?" Rowan asked as she stepped around him.

Brogan looked at Quinn, who'd remained suspiciously quiet during the little demo of his animal behavior. Their gazes connected and he could see the laughter in his best friend's eyes. The bastard knew this wouldn't be easy and if Quinn knew anything about him, he knew everything. As he knew Quinn. He wouldn't fool himself into thinking Quinn felt sorry for him. Oh, no. To Brogan's way of thinking, Quinn was looking forward to the inevitable fight to come.

EL WATCHED her best friend pull away from the man built like the side of a house. He was huge. She'd be lucky to come up to his shoulder, not that she'd get too close, something about him made her stomach churn and her heart pound.

The air in the room crackled with tension, thick with energy, the kind that spikes before a lightning strike. The skin that had tightened moments before she left her room now tingled, stretched, pulled tighter. Her hair stood on end and goose bumps broke out all over. She felt the need to strip off her clothes and rub herself all over the big man who still hadn't turned to face her.

Her eyes bored into the back of his head, even when Rowan reached her side and grabbed her up in another hug of welcome. Distractedly, El returned Rowan's affection and tried to ignore the slight desperation in it. She'd always been able to judge Rowan's moods and right now anxiety rolled off her in waves.

"I'm so glad you're finally here," Rowan said as she gave one final squeeze and let go.

El dragged her gaze away from the rigid man across the room and looked at her friend. Nothing could detract from the happiness etched all over the beautiful face in front of her. Rowan glowed and it went far deeper than the smile spreading her lips. Her eyes sparkled and she no longer had the pinched expression El had come to expect.

"I'm glad I came, too. Although if you'd mentioned how damn cold it would be I might have reconsidered," she joked. El gripped both of Rowan's hands and pulled her arms out wide. "Being home must really agree with you. I didn't say it earlier but you look gorgeous. But then you always do."

"Stop. You'll make me blush." Rowan let go of one hand and tugged her farther into the room. "Come and meet Quinn and Brogan, they just got home."

El hadn't noticed the second man earlier and as they got closer to the two men on the other side of the room her heart rate accelerated. A layer of sweat coated her skin and her breasts grew heavy, her nipples impossibly hard. Between her legs throbbed and went slick. With each shortened breath her nostrils were filled with the scents of open air, the rich, earthy aroma of the forest, and man. It was the last smell that had her nerves in overdrive.

The numbing cold she'd felt from the moment she stepped off the plane no longer existed. Instead her body burned with a heat unlike anything in living memory. Fire burst and consumed, leaving behind an arousal so great each step, each rub of her thighs took her closer to an orgasm that would be shattering.

What was going on? Sure she hadn't had sex in months but then she hadn't wanted to. Until now. Now she wanted to get down and dirty with the guy who still had his back to her. El's feet faltered and she stumbled. Rowan turned to glance at her, her eyes going wide when she caught sight of El.

Great. It was painfully obvious that her friend knew what had made El trip over her own toes. She felt her cheeks blush. She was already so hot with arousal they were probably day-glow red.

"Jeez, Brogan, turn it down." Rowan's words made no sense. "Here, let's go into the kitchen while my brother gets himself sorted out."

Doing an about-face, Rowan marched them back the way

they'd come. "Quinn, get him calmed down or make him leave," Rowan said over her shoulder as they cleared the doorway.

Dazed and confused, El let herself be led past the stairs and down a long hallway toward the rear of the house. Picture frames covered the walls, a perfect mixture of people, nature and animals. All the photographs showed Rowan's distinct style. One large photo caught El's attention. A lone coyote stood on a snow-covered hill, his body facing away, his head turned to look straight into the camera. He appeared to be posing for the person taking the shot.

A chill raced down El's spine. He seemed to stare straight at her as though he could see her. His gaze held her captive and she swung her head to keep him in her sights as Rowan pulled her past. Those yellow eyes followed her, and caught in some sort of trance, she twisted her neck to the point of pain, her eyes ensnared by his.

A door swished open and she was forced to turn, to watch where she walked or risk an injury. The second they stepped into the kitchen El was swamped with warmth. The room, large and bright, welcomed her with its cozy feel. Big windows covered the back wall, the view of the yard, forest and mountains in the background unobstructed. The winter sun reflected off the snow and lit up the huge room.

The big, granite-topped island in the center of the room held a sink and work area with four stools lined up on one side. Rowan pushed her onto one before heading to the wall of cupboards.

"Sit. I'll get us a drink, something warm, and we'll catch up."

El watched Rowan open a glass-paneled door, pull out two tall mugs and make her way to the coffeepot. She changed filters, scooped in coffee and flipped a switch, all her movements smooth and confident, so different from the woman El had first met. Oh, she'd seen an improvement in Rowan over the years they'd spent together but now she saw the woman that had been hidden inside. Strong, sure of herself, Rowan had finally grown comfortable with who she was and the world around her.

Something El wished she could be again.

BROGAN LET his muscles relax and his coyote subside. The beast was still wide awake but no longer threatening to pull free. Knowing what he was dealing with made things easier. He couldn't just take El and expect her to fall into line. If she was a shifter it would be easy but she wasn't. He wasn't even sure she knew what they were, never mind that he was one.

"You need to back off some."

Quinn's quiet voice pulled Brogan's gaze across to where his friend stood beside the fireplace. When had Quinn moved from the lounge? Normally he was aware of everything around him. Had El messed up his instincts so much that he failed to notice what went on next to him?

"I know. I just didn't expect it. I've never struggled to hold my control like that before. Was it like that for you?"

"Yeah. You get used to it and once you join it's not as bad."

"Jeez, no wonder you drove me insane all those years ago. Good thing you and Rowan finally sorted everything out."

"There was never any doubt as there isn't with you and El. But it'll be an interesting time between now and then."

Quinn's smirk had his hackles rising but Brogan knew he deserved everything the other man dished out. He'd given Rowan and Quinn plenty of crap while they had danced around each other before she'd been forced to leave home. Brogan sighed. Obviously it was his turn at the mating waltz.

"The problems won't just be between you and El," Quinn said.

"I know. But since I can't change who my mate is I'll just have to deal with what comes."

"The Council will have to be informed and there are those who will use El's non-blood status to undermine your position."

"I don't care about any of that. What I care about is making sure El doesn't freak out when she discovers we aren't exactly human."

"That might prove to be the easy part yet."

"I doubt any of this will be easy."

"Probably not, but we'll have to keep her from the pack until she understands, Brogan."

"Yeah, I'm more than glad you and Rowan decided on a small ceremony. El won't have to face anyone until after." Brogan didn't say after what, they both knew that until he turned El she couldn't be left alone or come in contact with any members of the pack.

"She'll be safe here but after the wedding we were supposed to take her up to the cabin. She wants to take wilderness photos for her next book. That gives you a week to convince her to stay and do what's necessary so she can."

"And if I can't convince her?"

Quinn shrugged. "You don't have a choice and you know it."

Brogan had no idea where to start when it came to wooing El. He'd never wooed a woman before. All he had to do was open his bedroom door and they fought each other to get inside. El would be different. For starters he had to tell her what he was without scaring her half to death and then convince her that he wasn't an animal when in essence he was.

The first step would be to actually meet her. The sooner they got used to each other the sooner they could get on with what had to be done. Hopefully Rowan was telling her who and what they were, but if not, he'd have to. He swallowed over the lump in his throat and rubbed the back of his neck. His muscles were tight—hard—but not from the beast wanting to break free.

No, now he was tense with nerves. If he didn't do this right he stood to lose more than his mate. He stood to lose his position as sovereign of the pack.

2

EL LISTENED to all Rowan had done since they'd parted almost a year ago. It was plain to see Quinn made her happy. She glowed from within. While Rowan talked, El said nothing. She wasn't ready to tell her friend what happened after she'd left. Wasn't ready to reveal the betrayal, the hurt, or her own stupidity. Trusting Ken had been the single dumbest thing she'd ever done. The price of that mistake had been high and Eloise had paid the price.

"I've babbled enough, what's been happening with you?" Rowan asked.

"Same old, same old. You know how it is," El hedged.

"What about the guy you'd started seeing? Ken? Are you two still going out?"

"Um, no. Things didn't work out the way I expected."

"Oh, come on, tell me all the details."

"Maybe later. For now I want to hear about what you've planned for your honeymoon." She changed the subject before Rowan could dig too deep into a wound that hadn't healed. Her heart hadn't been broken in the Ken debacle, she'd been ashamed of how little the nasty break-up had affected her heart. Finding him in bed with her assistant had hurt but finding her business accounts cleaned out of their funds had been far more devastating. El had come to the conclusion she'd never really loved Ken, it had been more of an in love with love thing. No, her heart hadn't been broken but her pride and self-confidence had.

El allowed Rowan's plans to fill her mind. With images of tropical beaches dancing in her head she almost forgot the hormones doing a two-step through her body. She even fooled herself into thinking she imagined the level of arousal she'd been caught in.

They'd finished their first cup of coffee when her temperature suddenly spiked and the air around her crackled. Her skin pulled tight, her nipples drew up into rock-hard nubs and moisture filled her panties. The pounding of her heart echoed in her ears and she swayed on her stool, lightheaded with the rush of blood through her body.

Rowan grabbed her arm and stopped her from toppling to the floor. Gripping the counter edge, El tried to take deep breaths. Her head cleared but blood roared in her ears, making her dizzy all over again. She knew before the door opened that he was coming. The hunk of testosterone from the front room. She knew with every quiver of her flesh he was the reason she turned into a boiling pot of lust.

"Are you all right?" Rowan asked.

She concentrated on the mug in front of her, tried to block out everything else and focus on the cup. El felt him enter the room, felt him back off but not leave. What the hell was with that? Rowan still had her by the arm, talking to her but she couldn't make out the words over the pounding in her ears.

With great effort El managed to speak. "I'll be all right. Just give me a second. Jet lag, I think."

"You need to go lie down, have a rest before lunch." Rowan slipped from her stool, pulling El up with her.

"I think you're right. A nap will do me good." El didn't think a nap would help anything but she needed out of the room and away from the man who crowded her without coming near.

She stood on wobbly legs, got her balance but wondered how the hell she was going to get upstairs without falling flat on her face. A cautious step had her knees shaking and her hand flying out to catch the edge of the counter again.

She caught something all right, something solid and warm but it wasn't the counter.

Fire streaked up her arm from her hand. She'd connected with his hip. Her fingers curled into the denim and held on. If she thought he generated heat at a distance it was nothing compared to the furnace he was up close. Every muscle grew soft. The air in her lungs evaporated and her mind went blank seconds before the world went black.

BROGAN HAD NEVER BEEN MORE thankful for his quick reflexes than now. El had barely begun the slide to the floor before he had his arm around her waist and her body snug against his. He looked over her head at Rowan.

"She fainted," he said.

The astonishment on Rowan's face mirrored his. Her mouth opened and closed, but no words came out.

"Did that ever happen with you and Quinn?" he asked.

"Once, but that was during a joining, not from just a touch." Quinn's quiet words came from behind him.

Brogan looked over his shoulder. "Is this normal?"

"Probably. You had some serious vibes going on before, but when her hand connected with you the heat just about singed *my* eyebrows." Quinn reached over and checked El's pulse.

Brogan knew her heart raced but it had slowed since she fainted. He altered his grip, scooted his arm behind her knees and swung her up against his chest. She couldn't weigh a hundred pounds, her bones were slight and there was a small amount of padding in all the right places. She was such a little thing. How could she possibly hold up against him?

The fear of what his strength could do to her sliced through him. How could he possibly hope not to hurt her? His needs were wild, and his need for her was greater than any he'd known. Arms trembling, he turned to face Quinn.

"She's so tiny." His words quaked with the anxiety exploding in his mind.

"Don't underestimate her, Brogan. El is tiny in stature but huge in courage," Rowan said.

"Rowan's right. Her inner strength is what you need to worry about and she's more than proven herself over the years they spent together."

He stared at Quinn, hoping he was right. Needing him to be right.

"Did you give her the back room? I'll take her up and sit with her until she comes around." At Quinn's nod Brogan stepped toward the door.

"No. I'll sit with her. I don't think her waking up with you in the room is a good idea." Rowan's soft footsteps followed him.

He knew she was right but he wanted to stay with El. No, what he really wanted was to take her to his room, lock the door and not let her out until she'd accepted who he was. Rushing things wouldn't get him anywhere, but the need to get there now warred with his need to protect her.

Rowan scooted around him and led the way upstairs.

Entering the bedroom had his senses tingling. Every part of the room felt touched by El. Her scent lingered in the air and her warmth filled all the corners. In less than two hours she'd stamped her claim on more than just him.

When Rowan pulled the covers back he lowered El's inert body to the bed, together they removed her shoes. She'd be more comfortable with her clothes off but he doubted she'd be happy waking up naked, especially with him in the room. There was no way he was leaving her no matter how much his sister protested.

He sat on the bed at El's hip and brushed the hair from her face. They didn't pull the covers over her as the central heating kept the room warm and he didn't want her to over-heat. Her face still looked flushed but her forehead was cool to his touch.

"You can go now, Brogan. I'll sit with her," Rowan murmured.

"I'm staying."

His sister chose not to argue, whether from the tone of his voice or the distraction of worrying about El, he didn't care. He wasn't leaving until she woke.

EL RUBBED her cheek against the fluffy pillow beneath her head. *Pillow?* She was in bed? The last thing she remembered was standing in the kitchen, telling Rowan she'd lie down for a while. She didn't remember coming up here.

Warm fingers smoothed her hair back. Startled, her eyes flew open and she pulled away. Two gold orbs stared back. They made her think of animals hiding in the bushes in the dead of night, but these eyes belonged to a very real, very large man. One who sat on her bed as if he had every right to be there.

"Easy, I won't hurt you." He continued to stroke her hair with steady, even sweeps.

"What...what happened?" Her whispered words had him leaning closer.

"You fainted, but you're okay. I didn't let you hit the floor." His gaze was hypnotic and strangely reassuring.

Warm breath fanned her face, filled her with the need to draw it in, take part of him inside her. She wanted to rub against the hand stroking her head. She didn't even know who he was.

"Who are you?"

"Brogan."

Rowan's brother.

The man who'd become an image in her mind. Strong, solid. Rowan had talked so much about him and Quinn over the years that El felt she knew Brogan even though they'd never met or spoken. He looked nothing like what her imagination had conjured up. This man was huge for a start and those eyes... She'd never seen that color in a human. Molten gold— simmering and swirling as if in constant flow.

She licked her dry lips, swallowed over the rawness in her throat. She'd been freezing since she arrived in the country but now her body was acting as if she were on Bondi beach in the middle of a heat wave.

"Do you want a drink?" Rowan's head popped up behind Brogan's shoulder. El hadn't realized there was anyone else in the room.

"Just a glass of water." Her tongue stuck to the roof of her mouth and her words came out as if the damn thing were four times its normal size.

"Be right back." Rowan disappeared, her footsteps echoing softly.

"Do you still feel dizzy?" Brogan asked.

Did she? No, not anymore, but she remembered the flash of heat just before everything went black. Her parched throat and tacky skin were signs that she hadn't imagined the burn she got from touching him. Where was that burn now?

"No, I'm feeling much better." She tried to sit up.

"Don't get up yet." With a hand on her shoulder, he pushed her back down.

"I was just going to sit," she protested.

"Oh, okay, hang on then."

He leaned over her and his chest brushed across her breasts, trailed over the tips, bringing them to instant attention. He grabbed a pillow from the other side of the bed and lifted her to tuck it behind her head, pressing her sensitized flesh into him. A shiver traveled down her spine.

"Now there's something I never expected to see. Brogan Wilder playing nursemaid." Rowan's laughter filled the room.

El's gaze fell on his face. Was he blushing?

Yes, his cheeks and neck had a tinge of pink in them. He pulled away and allowed his sister to pass her the glass of water. El couldn't help it; in great big gulps she tried to quench her arid throat and douse the fire springing to life inside her.

"Hey, hey, slow down." Brogan snatched the glass from her. "You'll choke if you're not careful. Just take small sips."

He held the drink to her lips and she tried to take it back but he wrapped his fingers around her wrist and pulled her hand away.

"I can do it myself," she huffed.

"Yes, you can, but I'm doing it for you and you're going to let me." His stern tone invited no further argument.

"Best to let him have his way, El, since he'll just make things harder if you don't," Rowan said as she headed to the door. "I'll be downstairs if you need anything."

El watched her friend go. She didn't want to be left alone

with Brogan but she couldn't think of a reason that she could voice and Rowan wouldn't leave her if he posed any real threat. She slowly turned to look at Brogan. The heat was still there but somehow not as scorching, not as frightening. The effect he had on her confused her more than anything. He was such a big man who exuded strength from every pore and yet somehow at the moment he seemed vulnerable.

Her gaze met his and he smiled. If she hadn't been turned-on before, she was now. That smile wasn't just toe-curling, it was panty-wetting. It held all sorts of naughty intentions and El wanted to strip herself bare and let him have at it. She'd never been overly sexual. Sex was nice but she didn't crave it. No other man had ever wiped her mind of everything but the need to consume and be consumed.

Brogan had her body coursing with sensations foreign to her, needs she had no idea she was capable of. Caught between common sense and baser urges, she wondered which way she'd go. She devoured him with her gaze, watched his eyes blaze with heat, heard his ragged breath grow shallow. He leaned forward, his lips inches from hers. Would he kiss her? Did she want him to?

Yes!

In the next breath Brogan closed the distance.

Heat lightning streaked through her, electrified every nerve, every cell. Her whole body screamed to be touched, stroked—possessed. Arching up, she slammed her breasts into his chest. Crushed against the wall of muscle, her nipples tingled and hardened, a line of fire darting from each straight to her throbbing core.

His tongue pushed against her lips and opening, she invited him in. The tangy taste of Brogan filled her mouth, her soul and she groped for his head, pulled him closer. Their tongues dueled—clashed—ought for control of a kiss that was all about greed. Teeth scraped against lips as each tried to get farther inside the other.

She pulled him down until the length of his body pressed into hers. She spread her legs wide, wrapped them around his hips and ground her sex on his. The hard ridge rubbed her clit, sent flames through her pussy and drew moisture from her core. Their hips pumped, mimicking the act their bodies craved. Over and over, his cock thrust against her clit, pushing her closer to the edge.

His hand slid between them and cupped a breast, lifting it. Fingers tweaked her nipple, tugged to the point of pain. Sensations splintered and El's arousal detonated. With blinding intensity she shattered into a thousand pieces. The one thing keeping her from flying away, keeping it all tied together was him. A hoarse cry tore from her throat.

"Brogan."

3

WHAT THE HELL was he doing?

Brogan held El in his arms as she came. Her body arched and bucked, shook with every spasm that rolled through her. They'd barely touched but she was so sensitive to his every move. Was that because they were mated?

He wanted to think it was him, wanted to think he was the only man to give her intense, instant pleasure.

With a final shudder, her body went soft beneath him. When had he moved on top of her, his body pinning hers beneath him?

Their mouths had pulled apart when El's orgasm broke and now they both dragged in great gulps of air. The harsh rasp of breath pumping in and out was the only noise in the room. Reality crashed in on him and he pulled back to look at her.

Her face, flushed with blood and slick with sweat, glowed with satisfaction. Her eyes fluttered open, unfocused and dreamy, they stared up at him. He shouldn't have touched her. She didn't know who he was, *what* he was, and before he had her she would have to know. He wouldn't be happy until he knew she came to him freely, knowing what she was getting.

"This shouldn't have happened. I'm sorry." Brogan scrambled up, got off the bed completely.

She stared at him, the dreamy expression gone, replaced with confusion. He knew the second it turned to anger. Her blue eyes turned glacial, slicing into him with their piercing stare. He swallowed the words bubbling in his throat, the ones that would soothe her and explain. The ones that would land him right back in bed when she wasn't ready for that yet.

"Why you—"

Her words cut off when she picked up a pillow and threw it at him. He ducked but it brushed his shoulder. "Eloise, please." A second pillow connected with his skull.

"Get out!" she screamed.

He held his hands up in surrender and backed toward the door. "Calm down, I'm going, but I'm warning you, this isn't over. I will be back."

She launched from the bed, picked up one of her missiles and charged at him.

"Calm down? Why you miserable, bloody—"

Thump!

Her weapon slammed into the back of his head as he turned. "Dammit, El, you'll pay for that later."

"And stay out!" Her shout was promptly followed by the slamming of the door.

He stared down at the raging hard-on in his pants. My God, she was magnificent angry. Her eyes shot fire and her cheeks flushed red. She wanted to beat him senseless and he wanted to *fuck* her senseless. If the whole thing wasn't so serious it'd be funny.

Footsteps echoed behind him.

"Off to a good start I see." Quinn chuckled, his eyes dropping to Brogan's groin.

"Don't say it. I screwed up. She probably won't talk to me for the rest of my life but I didn't fuck her. Not quite anyway."

"How can you not quite fuck her?"

"We kissed. Fooled around a bit," Brogan said before mumbling, "It's what happened after that got me in trouble."

"What happened?"

"Knock it off, Quinn. I'm not giving you the details of my sex life." What was with Quinn anyway? They hadn't had sex. He'd come crashing back to reality before things had gone that far.

"Did she orgasm?"

"What the fuck? What kind of question is that? And why the hell are you asking?" Brogan yelled.

"Because, dipshit, if she did by your hand, you marked her."

"I know that."

Quinn took a deep breath. "I'll ask a different way, is she marked?"

"Fuck!"

"I'll take that as a yes."

"Fuck!"

"You said that already."

"I know but... Fuck!" Brogan paced two strides away, two strides back.

"She can't leave the house. And she has to be told. The sooner the better."

Brogan knew Quinn spoke the truth. He ran his hand over his face. Why did it have to be so easy to mark your mate? "We tell her today. It can't wait."

"You can't just dump it on her. Not after she fainted and..." Quinn waved his hand in the direction of her door.

"Dammit, she has to know. And you said it yourself, the sooner the better."

"Fine, do it your way."

"Don't I always?"

"Yes, but somehow I think this time might be different."

"I may have marked her and placed her in danger but I'm here to protect her. Nothing will happen."

Quinn snorted. "It's not her I'm worried about. Get yourself sorted." He pointed at Brogan's still-hard cock. "I'll get Rowan to come up and check on El."

Brogan gave his friend a nod.

Quinn took two steps before adding, "If you're lucky, I won't tell your sister what happened."

Ah, shit!

Rowan was gonna kill him if she found out. "Don't tell her. It stays between you and me. Once El knows about us it won't matter, she's not going anywhere."

His gut tightened. She no longer had a choice. With one stupid kiss he'd taken it from her and now he'd never know if she stayed because she had to or because she wanted to.

"It'll work out, give her time. She feels what you feel, Brogan, she just doesn't understand it. Go cool down and I'll get Rowan to come check on her."

Quinn's sympathy did nothing to ease the guilt burning a hole in his gut.

The rattle of old pipes in the wall behind him broke the silence. El must have gotten into the shower. Images of her naked, slick with water and soap filled his mind, stirred his blood and made his dick even harder. He squeezed his eyes shut but couldn't stop his mind from picturing the woman on the other side of the wall.

Growling, he stalked to his room. It looked as if he'd be showering too—in cold water. Quinn's laughter followed him down the hall, grating on his already agitated nerves as Brogan stomped away.

He strode into the bedroom, ripping his shirt over his head and tossing it on the floor as he headed toward the bathroom. By the time he hit the cold tap, his pants were undone and halfway down his legs. In less than a minute he had his shoes off and his jeans following.

The pounding of water hitting tile drowned out the groan of frustration he couldn't suppress at the sight of his cock. He'd never had so little control. The beast had remained suspiciously quiet and Brogan had to wonder what that was all about. He hadn't felt it pulling to be free since he'd kissed El, since she'd come apart in his arms.

Damn!

He'd marked her. No wonder the beast had gone back to snoozing, it knew she was his. Stepping under the stinging spray, Brogan closed his eyes and raised his face, let the water stab his skin with its needle-like drops. His mind played over what he'd done, how she'd kissed him back with such demand.

Her need had been as great as his and when she'd shattered at his touch he'd been breathless with awe. She looked so beautiful flushed with arousal. Her eyes all dreamy, her lips plump from their kisses and her nipples hard as diamonds against his chest.

His cock twitched and oozed pre-cum. The cold shower did nothing to cool the blood boiling in his veins or the lust trampling on every nerve. He gave in, leaned back against the wall and grabbed his unruly cock in a tight fist.

Brogan imagined El in the shower, her soapy hands traveling over pink-tinged skin, down over her chest, across her taut stomach and between her legs, slow slides on smooth muscle and supple flesh. With eyes closed and head thrown back, she delved between her thighs. Her lips parted on a moan as she thrust deeper, riding her hand and the pleasure it gave her. With each stroke her hips moved, undulated against the fingers probing inside.

Teeth bared, Brogan increased his grip, moved his hand faster. The image in his mind stilled as her eyes opened wide to stare straight at him as she flew over the edge. He ground his jaw on a growl of satisfaction when she came for him—only him—and he followed.

Cum shot from the tip of his cock, dripped down his hand and onto the shower floor. He kept his movements hard and steady, milking every last drop of seed from his balls. Spent, he slumped against the wall, breathed deep and thought about going to her room and taking her.

No other woman made him lose control. He'd given in to an urge he normally controlled with an iron fist. Instead he had that fist wrapped around his cock as he fantasized about El getting herself off.

He'd come hard and fast but arousal rode his back like he hadn't. His prick, ramrod-straight and steel hard, didn't look as if it was going down anytime soon. She was his weakness, his Achilles' heel and if his enemies worked it out they'd use her to get to him.

He wouldn't allow it. He'd protect her, teach her to protect herself, but first he had to tell her, explain what he was and about the coyote ways. It was going to be a long couple of days. No point putting it off any longer. Brogan ran the soap over muscles still taut with tension. He stepped beneath the spray and rinsed before he flicked the water off and got out.

Ignoring the towels, he headed back into his bedroom. He yanked open drawers, got out a shirt and clean jeans and threw them on the bed behind him. He searched for a clean pair of socks but couldn't find any. Where the hell were they?

A gasp from the doorway had him whipping around and

coming face to face with a very shocked—and dressed—Eloise. Her mouth hung open and she didn't take her eyes off his prick, which had its eye pointed her way. Damn thing bobbed as if it was waving hello.

He cleared his throat and her gaze darted up to meet his. He waited to see what she wanted.

"I...um..."

Her neck and face red with embarrassment reminded him of how she looked when she came in his arms. She coughed and tried again.

"I... I wanted to apologize for before. Back in my..." She gestured over her shoulder. Before he could reply she continued. "I know it was as much my fault as yours and I agree that it shouldn't have happened. I can assure you it won't again." Her spine straightened and her shoulders pulled back with her last words.

Well now, wasn't it a shame that he had every intention of it happening again? And again. Time to let her know.

"El, there's no need to apologize and I'm taking back mine. I can also tell you that it will happen again, but not yet. There are things we need to talk about before we find ourselves in the same position."

Her hand flew up to cover her throat, her fingers trembling. He stalked toward her, uncaring of his naked state. Invading her personal space, he breathed deep and could still smell her arousal under the fresh layer of soap and shampoo. She may have tried to wash him off but he was still there, mixed in with the fragrance of her cream.

Oh yeah, she was marked all right. Marked as his. He couldn't wait to have her. All of her.

"Next time you come apart in my arms I'll be buried deep inside your tight body, nothing between us but the pleasure we'll give each other." He ran a finger along her jaw, tilted her head up to see her eyes. "Make no mistake, it *will* happen again."

Eyes wide she let him drag his finger over her lips. So soft. So plump and kissable. He lowered his head, brushed his mouth where his finger had been.

"Next time I won't stop," he breathed against her.

She gasped, her lips parted and a puff of minty-fresh breath filled his nostrils. He took advantage and thrust his tongue out, invading her mouth with hot licks and bold strokes. Her taste intoxicated him, flooded his senses and fueled his lust. He took the kiss deeper, devoured all she had to give.

He swallowed her moan before it left her throat as the urge to take, to possess stole through him. He pulled back and slowed the kiss until it was soft and lush. Breathing hard, she followed him when he broke their bond. Her whimper of protest echoed his.

"Not yet. Soon, but not yet." He breathed hard with renewed need. "There's too much to know, to learn, before I take you."

Her lust-filled eyes drew him in, made him want to break his own decree. He wanted to pick her up, slam the door closed and have her in his bed. The next few days would test his control a thousand times. He'd given it up once, but he wouldn't do it again. He couldn't let this slip of a woman break the one thing he prided himself on most.

The command he had over his needs, desires, and his position as sovereign. He couldn't afford to loosen the reins and show weakness because he could lose El, leadership of the pack and possibly his life.

4

EL SAT on a stool next to Rowan while Quinn and Brogan stood on the other side of the kitchen. She listened as Brogan issued orders for them to stay inside. Neither she nor Rowan was allowed to leave the house without one of the men. He went on about the weather and snowstorms that blew up unexpectedly, but she didn't think that was why he was forbidding them from venturing out.

She couldn't quite work out what exactly was up but that was the least of her worries. Rowan had just agreed without batting an eyelid. El's mind fought over whether to do as she was told or argue the point that she wasn't stupid and wouldn't get into trouble stepping out into the yard.

The undercurrents running between Brogan and Quinn had her worried. Something was going on beneath the surface and she wanted to know what made these two strangers think they could order her around. She knew whatever it was had to do with her but what could she have done to warrant being a virtual prisoner in this house?

"Okay, now that's settled I've got calls to make. I'll be in my office if you want me." Brogan strode from the room without another word.

Rowan's stool scraped along the floor and over El's nerves. She sat in stunned silence, unable to move or think past what had just happened. Why hadn't she protested? Had the man scrambled her brain so much with one orgasm? Sure it had been mind-blowing, the best she'd ever had to be honest, but she'd never allowed anyone to order her around before. Why start now?

A cup of coffee landed on the counter in front of her. Snapped out of her thoughts, she glanced up to find Rowan looking at her with concern and Quinn nowhere in sight. When had he left the kitchen?

"Are you sure you're okay? You still look a little pale, maybe you should go lie down until dinner." Rowan's forehead creased with worry and El felt bad for causing her friend any anxiety this close to her wedding.

"I'm fine, honest. Still tired but fine. There's nothing to worry about except getting all the final details of your big day finished." El smiled and hoped it reassured Rowan enough for her to stop fretting.

She suffered through a minute of continued scrutiny before Rowan nodded and went to get the folder with all the information for next Saturday. El didn't think there was anything left to do but they agreed to go over it one more time to be sure.

Three cups of coffee and two hours later, they were both satisfied everything was in place and excluding bad weather, the day would go off without a hitch.

She busied herself rinsing their mugs and stacking them in the dishwasher while Rowan puttered about behind her, pulling things from the fridge.

"Why don't you go watch some TV or read while I get

dinner started and then we can spend the rest of the afternoon relaxing," Rowan said.

"You don't want help?"

"No, you go on into the lounge room, the fire should be going and I think there are some magazines on the side table."

Rowan bumped El with her hip as she carried vegetables to the island counter. "Go." She made a shooing motion with her elbow. "I'll join you in a few."

El laughed. "Okay, I'm going but if you don't join me soon I'll come get you."

The whole scene reminded El of when they lived together, how easily they fit around each other. How Rowan had always tried to mother her and anyone else she could. Smiling, she entered the lounge room and found the fire roaring in the hearth, the room cozy and welcoming. She plopped down into a recliner and picked up a magazine with one of Hollywood's latest starlets splashed across the cover.

She had no idea how long she sat pretending to read the articles or why she couldn't get her mind off Brogan and his damn orders to stay inside. If he'd said nothing she probably wouldn't have wanted to go out, but because he'd told her she couldn't, her mind had decided she had to.

She felt trapped, suffocated. The house was warm and inviting but it made her itch to breathe fresh air. She wanted to suck the cold winter chill into her lungs and look up at the clear blue sky. Just sitting on the front steps would be enough to relieve the pressure constricting her.

Damn the man for making things difficult.

There was that little scene up in his room to consider too. She'd realized while showering she'd been equally to blame for what happened. At first she'd decided she should leave it alone but then the thought of tiptoeing around each other for the next week made her cringe and she had to apologize.

He'd stood there naked, all sculptured male perfection and her mind had emptied. Completely devoid of anything other than the urge to jump him and finish what they'd started. Even now she hummed with arousal and need. He had her going around in circles. How could she want him so much when she wasn't even sure she liked him?

El hated her indecision, hated the swinging back and forth between lust and loathing. She'd never been this mixed up. She needed to get outside. Needed to walk and think. Action always cleared her mind, gave the answers to her problems. Brogan certainly was turning into a problem. A big one.

Surely she could go out on the porch? She could walk the length of it and clear her head. Would it hurt to sit on the step and watch the world around her? Other than the quick look on the drive in she hadn't seen much of Whispering Springs and Rowan had told her so much about the mountains and her home at Whispering Creek Lodge that El wanted to see it through her own eyes. Just one look, that's all.

Snapping the magazine closed, she dropped it back on the table and pushed from the chair. He couldn't stop her from going outside. Not unless he tied her to her bed. A shiver ran down her spine as an image of Brogan tying her up flashed across her mind's eye.

It wasn't a shiver of fear.

"Grrrr!" Her teeth ground as her frustration built.

Walking down the hall, she put her head in the kitchen door where Rowan was busy washing lettuce. Taking advantage of her distraction El said, "I'm just going to sit on the front step for a bit, get some fresh air."

"Okay." Rowan's acknowledgement came just as El had hoped, without thought.

She backed out of the doorway.

If Brogan found out she'd gone outside he'd flip but what he didn't know couldn't hurt him, or in this case, hurt her. The man might be an "I'm in charge type" but El wasn't about to let him tell her what she could and couldn't do. She marched down the hallway to the front door, building up steam as she went.

Just because he was used to giving orders and people taking them didn't mean she had to. They'd only just met for God's sake. But what really got her mad was that even when he told her what to do or made her angry she was still attracted to him. Her brain might want to argue and tell him to go to hell but her treacherous body wanted to jump his bones.

How could her body betray her like that? And what happened to her spine? Had that bastard Ken done so much damage to her self-esteem? Well, no more. She wasn't about to let any man choose what she could and couldn't do. Or tell her where to go and not go.

El stormed through the front door, breathing hard and mumbling under her breath about tyrants and giving orders. At the last second she swung back, palm out and caught the solid oak panel before it slammed closed. Heaven forbid Mr. High and Mighty *hear* her disobeying one of his rules.

Who did he think he was? Standing there dictating what they could and couldn't do like some maniac despot ruling his subjects with an iron fist. She wasn't even all that pissed off that he'd given the orders. No, she was pissed because both Rowan and Quinn had gone along with him as if he should be obeyed in every way.

Don't do this! Don't do that! Christ, he'd be telling her when to come next.

El stumbled. One foot hit an icy patch of snow and she slipped, her legs separated and wobbled beneath her. Her arms flailed about until she got her feet back under her and caught her balance. Braced with her legs apart and her arms out wide like someone doing jumping jacks, she stood perfectly still and sucked in a breath of frigid air.

Was that what had her so agitated? He aroused her beyond belief and she wanted to do what he said. *Wanted* to please him.

She squeezed her eyes closed, breathed slow and deep and tried to steady her pounding heart and jittery nerves. He'd had her all riled up from the second they met, her body at once screaming for her to get away and get closer. El opened her eyes and continued to walk, taking care not to step on any more slippery patches of snow even though she wanted to stomp about to release the frustration bubbling inside.

A drop of moisture landed on her cheek, distracting her from her troubled thoughts. It was starting to snow. El tilted her face up to let the cold flakes bathe her skin.

It was such a magical scene. The view of the forest and mountains covered in a white blanket that shimmered as more snow fell from the sky was spectacular. The cold didn't just cool her body, it cooled her temper too. Taking the edge off enough for her to think rationally about what Brogan had asked and to see it from his point of view.

She couldn't blame him for being worried about her out here in unfamiliar territory. She'd never been here before and he had a right to be concerned she might get lost or hurt. But she wasn't stupid or incapable and wouldn't put herself at risk.

A sigh exploded from her chest. This was so unlike her, so completely out of character. She prided herself on her level-headed approach to life. Had the last few months done far more damage than she'd believed? Sure, she'd known her pride was dented, and her self-confidence had taken a blow, but this irrational attraction and anger coupled with confusion just wasn't her at all.

The snow sparkled as it floated to the ground, landing on

the path and trees, on El. She shuddered and wrapped her arms across her chest. She rubbed her hands from elbow to shoulder, trying to ease the chill and wished she'd grabbed her coat before leaving the house. The storm was getting worse.

Time to head back inside.

She turned and slipped, her hands flying out to stop herself from landing face first. Her fingers sank into the powdery cold slush. Pushing up, El stood and stared at the forest in front of her. The stumble must have turned her around. Gingerly, she spun around. More forest. Sucking in a breath, she twisted back again. Forest.

Oh God!

Slowly she rotated a full three hundred-sixty degree turn.

"Where's the house?" Her whispered words the only sound in the silence of the snowfall.

Oh God! Oh God! Where is it?

She stood still and turned her head to look over her shoulder. She stared straight ahead again, at where she thought the house should be. Was that gray shadow between the trees the house? With her eyes squinted it didn't get any clearer and the curtain of falling snow had grown heavier, causing the scenery to blur further. The shiver that went through her had nothing to do with the cold. Panic lodged in her throat. Fear clutched her heart.

Brogan was going to kill her. She'd done the one thing he'd told her not to and instead of proving she was capable of looking after herself, she'd proven him right.

Her body shook violently. This time it had everything to do with the cold. Her thin sweater was drenched on the shoulders and the sleeves weren't far behind. Her short hair stuck to her scalp, wet with snow that dripped onto her face. Her running shoes were soaking through and her toes had gone numb.

Her teeth chattered sending a jarring rattle through her

head. Her fingers and hands were stiff with cold and the knuckles ached. Wrapping her arms around her body, El tucked her hands under her armpits, trying to ease the throb. Now that she stood still and took stock of her body she realized her jeans were wet and getting wetter and she was halfway to frozen.

If she didn't work out which way to go soon Brogan would be the least of her worries. If she couldn't find the house, she'd freeze to death before he got to her.

BROGAN CAME up behind Rowan and pinched a slice of the cheese she was cutting for dinner. When he went for a second piece she smacked his hand away with the back of the knife.

"Stop it! You'll spoil your dinner."

"Dinner won't be for a couple of hours and you know nothing could spoil my appetite." He quickly snatched a second piece and darted to the other side of the kitchen.

"Brogan," Rowan warned.

"Okay, no more I promise." He held his hands up. His mood was light since he'd come to a truce of sorts with El. Plus, he'd made it clear she and Rowan were not to leave the house. Between now and the wedding he or his sister would find the right time to tell El about their heritage.

Yes, things were starting to come together.

"Where's El?" he asked.

"Out front."

"*What!*" he yelled.

"She's sitting on the front steps getting some fresh air." Rowan turned to face him, an eyebrow raised.

"Outside?" His voice had lowered but would still have been heard upstairs.

"That's where the front steps were last time I looked."

What the hell was wrong with her? How could she have let El leave the house?

"Jeez, Brogan, lighten up. She's just getting some air, not going on a mountain trek." Rowan shook her head and returned to cutting cheese.

For a second his mouth flapped but no words came out, then adrenaline kicked in and the beast sprang to life.

"Rowan!" he roared.

"What? Why the hell are you yelling at me?" She raised her voice but wasn't yelling.

"How could you let her leave the house? You both promised you wouldn't until after the wedding." He spun on his heel ready to charge through the front door and drag El back inside.

"For Christ's sake Brogan, she's just out front. Nothing's going to happen on our own porch."

Brogan stopped. He didn't want to tell her but he had to now. Had to so she'd understand El couldn't leave the house. He looked at her over his shoulder. "She's marked, Rowan."

"Marked?"

He nodded.

"You had sex with my best friend?" Her soft tone didn't bode well. Any second the explosion would come.

Sure enough, the knife she'd been using sailed past his head and embedded in the wall behind him. Most would say he was lucky she missed but Brogan knew luck had nothing to do with it, she had a true aim. If she'd wanted to hit him she would have, either between the eyes or through the heart. Rowan never missed a target.

"We didn't have sex. It didn't go that far."

"But you marked her!"

"I didn't mean to. It just happened and…"

Rowan flew past him into the hall.

Oh God, Eloise!

He tore out of the kitchen after her. Quinn came down the stairs as they headed for the front door.

"Where's the fire?" Quinn asked.

The door crashed back against the wall.

"El!" Rowan screamed.

"What the hell's going on?" Quinn was right behind him as Brogan hit the porch.

"El came out to get some fresh air," he ground between clenched teeth.

"What? When? Where the hell is she?" Quinn demanded.

"And when the fuck did it start to snow?" Rowan whispered.

"Where is she?" Brogan swung his head, frantically searching for El. There was no sign of her.

"I don't know. She said she'd just be here on the front step."

"Quinn, go in and get some gear." He pulled his sweater and shirt off together.

"Brogan, what are you doing?" Rowan asked.

"I'm going to find her. I'll bring her back if I can. If not I'll keep her in place until Quinn gets to us." He unbuttoned his jeans, pushed them down and yanked his boots off with them.

"Brogan, you can't go to her in your coyote form. You'll scare her to death." Rowan protested.

"I've got no choice. She'll freeze to death if we don't get to her soon."

Quinn came out the door, his jacket on, a pack thrown over one shoulder and El's jacket in his arms. "She didn't take her coat. We need to move now." He picked up Brogan's clothes and shoved them into the pack.

Brogan left the porch at a run as muscles stretched and bones popped. He bent forward and by the time his hands reached the ground they were paws. Shifting for him took no thought, no effort. In seconds he was sniffing the air and following El's scent along the path into the woods.

He heard Quinn running behind him, the distance between them getting greater with each stride. Nose down, he bounded down the trail and quickly disappeared from view. How had she managed to get so far? The storm was rapidly turning into a blizzard and his keen vision was the only thing keeping him from crashing into the trees.

His fur hung limp, wet from the snow and the sweat pouring out of him. He pumped his legs, his heart racing. The strain and pull on his muscles went unnoticed as he ran for all he was worth. The fear of not getting to her soon enough rode his back, made him push harder.

He left the path and was slowed by the density of the trees and thick underbrush. Why had she left the path? Burs caught in his fur. Brogan ignored them. He had to get to El, had to find her before she froze to death. Or worse, someone else found her.

The snow fell into his eyes, blurred his vision. His lungs burned but nothing except finding El would stop him. Her scent grew stronger, the wet conditions didn't hamper his senses but if it got any wetter it would wash her scent away completely. He had to find her before that happened.

Closer now, he slowed. She didn't need him barreling down on her in coyote form. He'd have to approach with care, not frighten her.

Two things hit him at once, the sight of El through the trees about thirty feet in front of him and another coyote between him and her.

· · ·

EL STARED at the wild animal in front of her. Teeth bared and hackles raised, he had obviously taken exception to her being in its forest. Well he wasn't the only one. He looked scrawny, his coat ratty and dull but what did she expect? A well groomed canine?

"Nice doggy, good doggy." Hands in front she backed away. He followed.

The grumble vibrating up his throat stopped her cold. Without moving her head, she searched the area, looking for anything she could use as a weapon to protect herself. He wasn't big, had to weigh less than she did. If she could find something to bash him over the head with there might be a slim chance she'd get to freeze to death after all.

She tried not to think of how else she might die. Those pointy yellow teeth sent icy fear skating through her veins. Saliva dripped from his curled lips and El's flight impulse kicked in. The urge to run, to turn and run, shuddered over muscles rigid with fear, but she didn't move. To do so would mean certain death.

One paw moved forward as a back one followed. With infinite care he walked toward her. He snarled wider, showed more of his menacing jaws. He was stalking her and all she could do was stand there. Wait for him to get closer. She might be able to kick out with her foot if he came within reach without lunging for her throat. How far could he jump?

When he got within twenty feet his snarl turned into a gut-stealing growl, teeth mashing together as he snapped at her. His legs bent and his chest dipped and she knew this was it, he would attack her now and it would be a fight for her life.

She braced her legs apart, bent her knees and bounced on the balls of her feet. All the things she'd been taught in her self-defense class. El figured she could get a good solid kick into his throat if he jumped the right way. If not she'd plant her foot in the first thing it connected with.

The coyote leapt and all her muscles tightened, ready to spring up.

She never got the chance.

With a spine-tingling howl, another coyote pounced. At first she thought it was coming for her as well, but when the newcomer took out the first one in a swift bone-crunching tackle she knew it was time to run. Blood sprayed across the pristine white snow and El's stomach turned.

She would not vomit.

Sprinting to the left, she took off. Trees and bushes slapped at her but she didn't stop. Her heart pounded in time with her feet, her toes squelched in her wet sneakers and her chest burned with each ragged breath. She needed to hide. She'd never outrun the coyote if he gave chase and she was sure he would.

El scanned the area as she ran, looked for anything that might conceal her. There was only one option. The last time she'd climbed a tree hadn't turned out well but if it was the difference between life and death, she'd do it. Spotting one that looked as if it would be easy to climb, she headed straight for it.

Bark dug into her palms as her fingers wrapped around a low branch. It took one tear in her jeans, numerous bruises and two attempts to get her legs over the limb. Her sweater caught as she swung up and she teetered on the verge of falling. The sound of pounding paws gave her renewed strength to throw herself up and out of reach.

The big gray coyote walked between the trees, his coat glossy and thick, his gait regal and confident. El held her breath, prayed he wouldn't see her. He stopped four feet from the base of her tree and without hesitation looked up at her.

She gasped as her hold slipped and a gouge ripped in the flesh of her hand.

It was the coyote from the photo.

Casually, as though he hadn't just attacked another animal, he sat on his haunches. His golden eyes watched her and, like with the photo, El was mesmerized, helpless to look away. From one heartbeat to the next she relaxed and knew without a doubt that he wouldn't hurt her.

Why she would think such a thing about a wild animal couldn't be explained but when he lay down on his belly, head on his paws, she felt no threat from him.

Curled on the branch, her numb body began to slide. Her shivering had come back now that the adrenaline was wearing off and her eyes drooped. She was so tired, she wanted to put her head down and sleep. But she knew she couldn't, not in the tree anyway. Falling was not an option. She'd break something for sure.

She climbed down from her perch. Careful not to startle the coyote with any quick movements, she eased to the ground and sat with her back against the trunk. With the danger passed, her body came alive with pain, cold and fatigue. Keeping an eye on the coyote, El waited for an attack in case she'd misjudged him. It never came. He watched her with unblinking eyes.

Feeling safe but tired, she bent her legs and hugged them to her chest. Closing her eyes she lowered her forehead to her knees as bone-rattling shakes swamped her. Her arms and legs went numb and her teeth chattered. She didn't flinch when the coyote sat next to her. Too exhausted, El had no strength left to move more than her head, she opened her eyes to look at him.

He was warm. His fur so soft she wanted to burrow into him and sleep. In the back of her mind she knew what she was doing was insane. She sat with a wild animal at her side but she wouldn't move. *Couldn't* move. His actions spoke of care and protection. He'd stopped the other coyote from attacking her and now he was keeping her warm, standing guard. And she was so sleepy.

The cold had her thinking and doing things she wouldn't under normal circumstances. Obviously she was hallucinating, in the throes of hypothermia or something. He rubbed his head back and forth on her arm. The motion soothed and reassured her he didn't intend to hurt her. If she died out here in this frozen wonderland at least she wouldn't be alone.

Lethargic with cold, she slumped against him. His coat encouraged snuggling and she buried her hands in his fur. Her cheek lay on his neck and she closed her eyes and enjoyed the heat he gave off. His heartbeat set a steady rhythm beneath her ear and lulled by his warmth and comfort, El draped her body over his.

She must have dozed because she didn't hear anything until Quinn stood in front of her. He dropped to his knees beside her, tossing a bag at her feet.

"Here, get changed. We need to get her back fast."

Confused by his words, El tried to get up.

"Not you, El. Let's get your coat on." Quinn gently eased one arm into the thermal garment.

Cold air flowed over her side as the coyote stood. She turned to watch him walk away, expected him to leave now there was another person here. But he didn't. With grace he walked a few feet away and before she could understand what she saw, Brogan stood before her. Naked.

Oh, my God! She was hallucinating. She did not just see that gorgeous animal turn into Rowan's brother. He reached for the bag Quinn had brought and pulled clothes out. Dressing quickly, he returned to her side just as Quinn got her zipped up.

"Brogan?" she whispered, the word full of the confusion swirling in her head.

"Shh... It's all right. I've got you now. We'll get you home and warm." He pulled her close and hugged her tight before he picked her up and started walking through the falling snow. El curled into his body and gave up the fight to stay awake.

6

HER FACE TUCKED into his neck sent shivers down his spine. She was cold as ice. The shaking had stopped while he lay against her in coyote form and now as he held her against his human body he knew there was no time to waste. He'd have to send Quinn to clean up.

"Quinn, over on Whispering Ridge is a coyote." He wouldn't need to explain further.

"Is he dead?"

"I don't know. El took off and I had to go after her."

"Okay, I'll see you back at the house."

As his best friend, Quinn could be trusted to do what needed to be done. As regal, Quinn held the position of Brogan's second and his loyalty was expected.

In the two years he'd held sovereign nothing had been easy. There were members of the pack who thought as a half-blood he had no right to the position. He'd like to think his skills and progress with pack finances and the more stable community proved them wrong.

The human in his arms could destroy all he'd achieved. No

one liked outsiders, especially non-bloods. Even after he turned El, gave her the ability to shift, she'd always be a non-blood. Could he expect her to go through life being looked down at? Did he have a choice?

Could he let her walk away if that was what she wanted? She was his mate, for him there would be no other. Could he live without her? Let her leave him and go on with her life, unprotected and maybe with someone else? She was marked as his and no matter where she went other shifters would know it.

No. If she couldn't live here with him, he'd leave with her. He'd walk away from all he'd known for her. Convince her they were meant to be together. But there was no point thinking about it now. They'd cross that bridge when and if they came to it. For now he had to concentrate on getting her back to the house.

He had no idea how long he trudged through the falling snow when the house came into view. The storm had almost reached whiteout and it was no wonder El had lost her way. Even he'd struggle without his natural coyote senses.

Rowan opened the door as Brogan came up the path.

"Upstairs. I've got blankets warmed and hot drinks ready."

"She's unconscious, the drinks can wait." He angled through the door, careful not to bump El's head on the frame.

Two at a time, he raced up the stairs. Rowan had turned up the heat because it got hotter with every step he took. At the top he turned toward his room.

"Brogan, you're going the wrong way," Rowan said.

He ignored her.

By the time he reached his bedroom sweat was beading on his skin but El needed the warmth so he wasn't about to complain.

He placed her on her feet. With one arm wrapped around her waist he started to pull her out of her wet clothes.

"Help me get her undressed," he barked.

"Okay, then I'll get the blankets from her room."

Between them they got El stripped naked. With one hand he ripped the covers off his bed and waited for Rowan to bring the blankets.

"Lay one on the bed," he ordered.

He was being blunt to the point of rudeness but his first priority was getting El warm. He'd apologize later.

When Rowan got the first blanket down, he laid El on it. *Christ!* Her skin was blue. He let Rowan cover her while he stripped out of his wet clothes. Body heat would be the best way to bring her temperature back up and he had every intention of sharing his.

"What are you doing?"

"I'm getting in with her. Body heat, Rowan, it's the best way." Lifting the blanket edge he climbed in and pulled El against him.

"She's so still. Maybe we should take her to the hospital."

"The storm is getting worse. We can't take her or we'd be risking all our lives. We just need to get her warmed up." Brogan hoped he was making the right decision.

"Where's Quinn?" Rowan asked.

"He'll be here soon."

"That's not what I asked, Brogan. Why didn't he come in with you?"

"He had to do something for me."

"What?" Tension laced her voice.

"Not now. After we get El warm I'll explain everything."

"But—"

"Later." He still wasn't sure what—if anything—they'd tell Rowan or El. It would all depend on what Quinn found on Whispering Ridge.

El lay motionless beside him. He covered her and tucked

the blanket around them to keep their body heat trapped. Her breathing was so shallow he couldn't feel her chest rising but he kept his fingers on her pulse point to assure himself she was still alive. He willed her to warm up.

Curled around her as best he could without crushing her, he clenched his teeth against the chill of her flesh. He may as well be hugging a snowman.

By scant degrees her temperature rose. She remained still in his embrace even as her skin lost the blue tinge that had scared him into thinking he'd been too late getting her home.

Sweat broke out on his back, his chest. The cocoon he'd made slowly turned into a furnace. He wouldn't last much longer in here with her. A few more minutes and then he'd get out and dress. The blanket, damp along his back from his sweat would have to be changed, too.

Rowan had disposed of their wet clothing before returning to sit in the chair near the window. Her gaze darted between watching for Quinn and checking El. Brogan knew she was torn between her dual worries. Her mate hadn't returned and the storm had finally become full whiteout conditions.

"He's back!" Rowan sprang from her perch and raced from the room.

Brogan's cue to get up and dressed. He wanted to know what Quinn had found. He hoped it wasn't what he thought it had been. Gently, he slipped his arm out from under El. She moaned and rolled over to follow him. Her hand reached out and grazed his chest, a nail scraping his nipple. The small bud hardened and his cock throbbed with arousal.

He'd managed to keep his desire for El at bay while he held her naked body, but in the back of his mind it was there. Waiting for the slightest move to bring it bounding out of the corner to take over his every thought, his every breath. He hated himself for wanting her when she was so sick and hated that they were in this situation at all.

She curled into a ball as a moan slipped from her lips and tormented his sensitized nerves. He grabbed a new blanket from the pile Rowan had left on the end of the bed. Draping it over her, he tucked the sides in. He pushed her hair from her face and ran his fingers through the damp strands. She settled at his touch, murmured and snuggled deeper into his bed.

Happy to see her face had lost its gray-blue tinge and her skin felt warmer beneath his fingers, he turned to get dressed. Pulling jeans and a shirt out, he quickly put them on. He could hear Rowan and Quinn coming up the stairs and from the tone of their hushed voices they were arguing. He smiled. Quinn was not giving up any more information than Brogan had.

"How is she?" Quinn asked as he came into the room.

"Warmer. She hasn't woken yet. Stirred a little when I got out of the bed just now, but that's all." Brogan walked over and placed the back of his hand on her forehead. Definitely warmer.

"Is someone going to tell me what happened out there?" Rowan demanded.

His sister wouldn't give up until she knew every detail. "I'm not sure yet. Let Quinn tell us what he found first and then I'll have a better picture."

"He was a natural. Old and starved half to death. I don't think he would have had the strength to do El much damage. He certainly didn't have enough to fight you."

"Damn."

"Yeah. There's more."

Brogan's head snapped around to look at Quinn. He didn't need to hear the words. He knew what Quinn would say.

"Marcus turned up while I was burying the body. He's

reporting you to the Council." Quinn didn't look happy about his run-in with Marcus.

Marcus was full-blood and thought he should hold sovereign but the man was an idiot of the first order and his leadership skills started and ended with intimidation and scare tactics. Not the type of leader any pack would want—or need.

"He can report me. I've done nothing wrong. I took the threat away with as little force as possible. The only thing I'm guilty of is leaving him there and going after El. But under the circumstances, that's acceptable," Brogan said.

"Yes, but we all know Marcus will put a spin on it," Rowan chimed in.

"He can, and I can front Council, explain what happened and if they still think I should step down as sovereign I will. But I think Marcus might be forgetting one thing. If I step down, Quinn, you take over." Brogan was thankful for that little bit of pack law.

"Does that mean we can expect him to try to kill Quinn again?" Rowan's voice quivered with fear.

"He can try but he won't succeed." Steely determination filled Quinn's words.

"He won't get away with it like last time, Rowan. We might not have been able to prove his involvement before but this time we know what and who we're dealing with," Brogan said.

It had cost them all to let Marcus get away with his involvement in the attempt on Quinn's life but as sovereign and regal their hands were tied by pack law. Next time Marcus did something, they'd make sure they had proof to take to the Council.

Or Brogan would ignore the law and go after him anyway. He'd keep that to himself though. No point worrying Rowan any more than she already was.

"Quinn, go get out of those wet clothes. We'll work out

what to do about Marcus after El wakes. There's not much we can do with the storm anyway," Brogan said.

"I'll get dinner in the oven. I think we could all use something warm to eat." Rowan leaned over El and checked the warmth of her skin with her palm. "She should wake soon, shouldn't she?" she asked.

"I think so. But she'll be tired as well as hypothermic. She's warmer now and that's what counts." Brogan sat on the edge of the bed, brushing his fingers lightly over El's cheek and pushing the hair off her face.

He waited for Rowan to leave the room. "Do you think Marcus was behind the natural's attack on El?"

"Hard to say but I wouldn't put it past him."

Brogan wouldn't be surprised to find Marcus had somehow been involved but how would he know El had gone wondering off unless he was watching the house? There would be no room for secrets now, with Marcus prowling around and stirring up trouble they would all need to be careful. Especially El.

"We can't afford to wait any longer. We'll have to tell her everything when she wakes. With Marcus causing trouble with the Council she'll need to know what's going on." Quinn voiced what Brogan had already decided.

When El woke, they'd tell her everything. What they were and what danger they were in from a man bent on gaining sovereign.

EL WOKE with a start and a cry of pain. Every muscle and bone ached.

"Easy. You're safe now." The deep voice rolled over her.

Brogan.

She opened her eyes, the low light of the room sending

prickles of pain into her skull. Tears formed, blurring her already limited vision.

"Where..." Her throat felt dry and scratchy.

"Here, drink some warm tea."

Brogan lifted her head, held a mug to her lips and she sipped at the sweet liquid. He kept her from drinking too fast, tilting the cup away after each sip. For the second time today she found herself on the receiving end of this hard man's gentle care.

After a few sips he took the cup away and placed it on the bedside table. Her eyes had adjusted to the low light and El could see that she was in Brogan's room. In his bed. He propped a pillow behind her back and she leaned into it, letting the softness cushion her sore body.

"I hurt," she whispered.

"You will for a while. You were awfully cold when I found you." The low soothing rumble of Brogan's voice shivered over her skin.

She wasn't feeling cold now. Her body was heating quickly as she began to wake further. She could smell snow and forest and Brogan. For someone who could describe a photograph with vivid words, she was at a loss as to which ones to use for his scent. It was hot and male, all Brogan.

"Are you still cold?" he asked.

"No."

No, she certainly wasn't. If anything she was rather hot. She pushed the blanket down in the hope of cooling off a bit. Brogan's drawn-in breath had her gaze darting to his face. He was staring at her chest. Looking down she found out why. She was naked. Where had her clothes gone? Who'd taken them off?

Scrabbling for the cover, she pulled it back up but the

damage was done. He'd seen her breasts and her pointy nipples. He had to know they weren't hard from being cold.

"What happened to my clothes?"

"They were soaked. We had to get you warm quickly. We took them off and used body heat to warm you up," he explained.

"Body heat?" Oh God, please no.

Brogan's devilish smile was all she needed to know the body heat had been his. Never mind seeing her naked, he'd been wrapped around her.

Her face flushed with arousal—or was it embarrassment? She couldn't decide which. The thought of being in Brogan's arms with not a stitch on had her hard nipples throbbing and her pussy watering. She closed her eyes and groaned. Would she always be in a state of confusion with this man?

"Don't worry, El. I behaved myself. Besides, when I don't behave I want you fully aware of everything I'm doing to you. No offense, but you brought new meaning to the words *cold fish in bed.*" His deep chuckle had goose bumps rising on her skin.

"How did I get here?" She tried to remember what had happened but her mind wouldn't clear and the only thing she could remember was losing sight of the house.

"I found you and brought you home." He was back to brushing her hair off her face, the motion soothing and arousing. Everything the man did seemed to turn her on.

"But I couldn't see the house. The snow…"

"I know, I warned you that the storms could blow up quickly out here."

She'd been standing in the snow looking around at nothing but forest when she'd heard heavy breathing behind her.

"The coyote!" she gasped.

"It's okay, he can't hurt you now," Brogan reassured.

"No. Not the wild one, the one from the photo downstairs." Her gaze met Brogan's and she knew before he said anything that what her mind was now remembering was real. It hadn't been a vision.

"Oh, God," she whispered, pulling away.

"I'll never hurt you." Brogan's words were gentle but full of conviction.

"You...you..." El couldn't say it, couldn't voice what she was thinking.

"I need to explain but I want Rowan and Quinn here when I do. What we have to tell you will be a shock but you have to know that none of us would ever hurt you or put you in danger." Brogan got off the bed and went to the door. "I'll be back in a second. I'll just get them so you can know the truth."

The truth? What truth? That he'd somehow turned from a coyote into a human? Human? Jeez, if he'd turned into a coyote he wasn't human. What did you call someone that was an animal one second and a human the next?

El laughed out loud, the slightly hysterical sound bouncing around the room. What had she gotten herself into?

7

"YOU'RE AWAKE." Rowan ran into the room and plopped on the bed next to her.

El looked at her and tried to decide if she could change form like Brogan. Her friend didn't look any different than she always had and nothing about her pointed to her not being human. Of course Brogan looked completely normal too.

"I was so worried. You scared us all half to death. Don't ever do that again," Rowan admonished.

"Can you..." Again the words stuck in El's throat.

Rowan grabbed both her hands and squeezed her fingers. "I'm sorry I never told you, but it's not exactly something that comes up in everyday conversation." She shrugged.

El had to agree with her. In fact she couldn't think of how it would ever come up in a conversation.

"El, I need you to hear me out. When I'm finished you can ask any questions you want and I'll answer them," Brogan said as he sat back on the bed.

Quinn stood behind Rowan. She scrutinized both of them closely but couldn't see anything to raise her suspicions. She turned back to look at Brogan. Nothing made her think they were anything but human.

With a nod she said, "Okay, I'll listen."

"We're what are called shapeshifters. We can change from human form to coyote. We're not the only kind of shifter but for now I'll just explain about us." His hand waved to indicate Rowan, Quinn and himself, which answered her earlier question. They could all change shape.

"There are two ways to become one. You're either born with the ability to shift or turned by a shifter. We were all born shifters but there are those in our community that have been turned. Once a human is turned they are able to shift form with practice but they're still considered non-bloods by our pack and inferior by some.

"Some shifters are referred to as half-bloods and others full-bloods. Some believe that half-bloods are as inferior as non-bloods, but those are feelings I aim to change. As sovereign, I'm working toward bringing our people together and forming a stronger connection that will enable us to continue to live among humans without detection." Brogan's last words held the strength of his will to achieve his goal.

"In every way that counts, we're human, El. We think and feel exactly the same, but we can change into coyote form when we want to," Rowan explained.

"There's one other significant difference between us and humans." Quinn's words drew El's gaze to him. "We mate for life. It's not a choice we logically make. When we meet our mate our bodies know and the result is a strong physical attraction that can be unbearable until we join for the first time."

"Once you meet your mate there is never anyone else. It's not something we can change," Brogan continued. "When mates are together they're marked, meaning all other coyotes know who you belong to. The mark works both ways, for the male and female.

"This can cause problems when the mate isn't a shifter." Brogan took her hand in his. "A human must learn about us and our ways before being turned and the choice should be theirs, not the shifters. Once a mark is made, it cannot be removed."

"This can be dangerous in a number of ways. As a human if you don't know you're marked and go into another shifter community you risk being physically attacked but you're also at risk from natural coyotes." Rowan's gaze was sympathetic. "Brogan marked you this morning."

El's gaze snapped to Brogan and her mouth hung open in shock.

"I have no excuse to offer for what I did, El." His Adam's apple bobbed as he swallowed hard. "Because of my lack of control I've taken your choice from you. You have no option now. You have to accept me as your mate."

"But...you said a human mate could choose whether or not they wanted to be turned."

"Yes, and you still have that choice but you have to take me as your mate. I can't allow you to go unprotected. If you don't want to be turned I won't turn you but I can't let you go. I'll leave Whispering Springs if that's what you want," he offered.

"I don't understand."

"I think what Brogan is trying to say is that he's prepared to leave Whispering Springs with you to live in Australia. You still have choices but he's taken away your option of not being tied to him," Rowan said.

"Okay, so I can choose to be turned or not but I can't choose to deny my mate? Is that right?"

"Yes."

"Yes."

Brogan and Quinn spoke at once.

El squeezed her eyes shut and laid back on the bed. This was so unreal. There were so many things to take in and she knew whatever happened her life would never be the same. Taking a deep breath, she opened her eyes and looked at Brogan.

"Will you do something for me?"

"Anything."

"Show me."

"Now?"

"Yes." As an afterthought she added, "Please."

She watched as he stood and began removing his clothes. Without a sign of discomfort at getting nude in front of Quinn and Rowan, he stepped back from the bed and as he bent to the floor, he changed from Brogan to coyote. It happened so fast she barely saw the change. One second he was Brogan the next he wasn't.

"Does it hurt to change?" she asked.

"No, but the first few times drain you of energy," Quinn explained.

"Does he understand what I'm saying?" El watched Brogan but continued to ask Quinn her questions.

"Yes, we still think as we do in human form but we have the added instincts and skills of the coyote body. We're exactly the same just in a different physical shape."

"How do you turn a human?"

Brogan growled but the sound didn't frighten her. Smiling she held out her hand for him to lick. He came closer, running his tongue over her outstretched palm before leaping onto the bed to stand over her and nuzzle the side of her face.

"I think I'll let Brogan explain about turning a human. You might want to ask him to change back now. He won't until you do." Quinn pulled Rowan to her feet. "We'll leave you alone for a while. You need to make a decision so we can deal with the pack Council."

"What Council?" El asked.

"We'll explain about it later. For now you need to talk to Brogan and make your choice," Quinn closed the door behind them as they left.

Brogan's coyote form lay next to her on the bed, his head resting on her stomach. Beneath the blanket El remained naked and the tickle of his warm breath fanned out over her belly. She remembered Quinn's comment about mates having an unbearable attraction until they joined. It explained why she'd been a bundle of lust since meeting Brogan.

"Oh, Brogan. What are we going to do?"

He whined, reminding her she hadn't asked him to change back yet.

"Change back, please."

She expected him to get off the bed but he didn't. He simply changed to human form and remained with his head on her stomach.

"I can't tell you what to do, El. I know what I want you to do but I also know what I've forced you to accept. I'm not sorry you're mine." He ran a finger along her jaw, up and across her lips.

Fire ignited from his touch and streaked through her body, leaving her in no doubt that they had an incredible attraction.

"Why aren't you freaking out about what I am?" he asked.

El smiled. "I guess my lifetime love affair with all things mythical helps me to accept it. Of course it doesn't hurt to have seen it with my own eyes." She laughed. "You know I've dreamed about creatures of myth and legend for most of my life and devoured every written text about them I could get my hands on. Maybe I knew I'd need it one day."

"Maybe." He toyed with a strand of hair.

"How do you turn a human, Brogan?"

"There are a couple of ways to do it."

"A couple?"

"Yes, but the most successful way is by joining." He tugged lightly before tucking the lock he held behind her ear.

"Meaning?" She thought she knew but wanted to hear him say it.

"Sex, El. I'll be able to turn you when we have sex." Surely there was a little more to it than that. After all, he'd said they could be mated without her being turned.

"So how did you mark me?" she asked.

"I wasn't thinking clearly and you kind of took me by surprise with how responsive you are. When I made you come earlier I marked you as mine." He trailed a finger around the shell of her ear.

"I didn't make you come so you're not marked."

"No. But I don't need to be marked to know I'm yours."

"You don't want me to mark you?" Had she misunderstood him?

"More than my next breath but it isn't my choice to make."

"I'm getting tired of all these choices, Brogan. Do you want to be mated with me or not?" Her frustration with him and the situation grew.

"Yes."

"Then turn me," she said.

"I don't need to turn you to be your mate, El. It's two different things."

"Okay, so what happens if we mate but you don't turn me? Am I able to live here with you without being able to shift?" She needed to be clear on this because once the decision was made there would be no turning back. Not that there was any going back now but she still wanted to understand.

"No. The shifter community would never accept you and I

would be forced to give up my position as sovereign. If you choose not to be turned we would have to leave here."

"So if I choose to be your mate but not a shifter we leave. If I choose not to be either, we leave. Is that right?"

"Yes."

"And you would do that, even if I don't accept you as my mate?"

"Yes."

"Why?"

"Because you're my mate and without you I'm not whole."

"Even if we aren't mated?" El struggled to understand what he was saying. He couldn't love her—he didn't know her. But he would sacrifice everything for her regardless of her decision. He said he'd taken away her choice but he'd also taken away his own. By being her mate he was forced to go along with what she chose, forced to leave his home and life to follow her. They were both out of choices.

"Brogan, what you've just told me shows that we both no longer have a choice in what we do. No matter what I decide you will be affected and so will I." She reached out and ran her fingers through his thick black hair, the silky curls twisting over her skin. "Are you a good sovereign?"

"I've made some improvements and stopped all of the fighting between the shifters living in and around Whispering Springs." Pride over his accomplishments shone bright in his eyes.

"Would they suffer if you left?" He turned toward her hand when she stroked down the side of his face.

"No. Not if Quinn stayed but I don't know if he and Rowan would stay without me here."

"What do you want to do? Do you want to stay in Whispering Springs?" El watched his eyes, wanted to be sure he told her the truth.

"I want to be with you. Wherever that is," he said.

"That's not what I asked, Brogan."

"This is my home. I was born in this house, in this room. I wouldn't leave it for anything but you."

"Then our choice is made. And it is our choice. It will have an impact on both of us." She covered his mouth with her fingers when he started to speak. "For me, moving here wouldn't be that big a deal. I have no family ties in Australia and I can work on my nature books anywhere that has internet access and a phone. For you to leave here you would be letting the shifter community down and walking away from the only life you've ever known. I couldn't live with you giving all that up. The guilt would eat at me. I can't ask you to make that sacrifice and I won't. My choice is made. Turn me, Brogan."

8

CONFLICTING EMOTIONS BOMBARDED BROGAN. Relief at El's acceptance of who he was, *what* he was, lifted the weight he'd been carrying in his chest. Elation at being able to claim his mate flowed through him, sparking his arousal and need to possess. And fear. Knowing what was involved in turning a human and actually doing it were two different things.

A coyote should only turn a human once—if at all—and never outside a mated pair. Icy tingles traveled his spine and the muscles in his stomach clenched tight. He knew how to turn El. Knew the instinct to do so would come naturally when they joined but fear of causing her pain had him breathing hard and sweat popping out on his forehead.

He wanted to flip her over onto her knees and take her. Claim her as his forever. He'd never been nervous about taking a woman to bed but El was different. Having sex had nothing to do with claiming your mate.

"Brogan?" El's voice drew him out of his thoughts.

He had to tell her there was more to being turned than just

fucking. She needed to know that he'd have to bite her, allow his coyote teeth to extend and sink into the soft flesh of her neck.

"El." He gulped over the hard ball lodged in his throat. "I, um…" Stammering like an idiot, Brogan searched his mind for the best way to explain what he had to do. "To turn you I have to bite you at the exact moment we both climax."

"Bite me?"

She hadn't backed away from his touch and still ran her fingers through his hair. He took that as a good sign.

"Yes, I need to use my coyote teeth to pierce your neck. I'm told it doesn't hurt because of the endorphins and hormones produced by our mating but I've never turned a human so I can't be sure. I don't want to hurt you." His blood ran cold and pain sliced into his heart at the idea of El suffering in any way.

"Brogan, I know we don't really know each other but I trust you. I know you'd never intentionally hurt me."

"I don't want to unintentionally hurt you either," he said. He'd never been this nervous or fearful.

"We don't have to do this now do we? Can't we spend some time getting to know each other? I want to know about Whispering Springs and your life. Will you tell me?"

Brogan took a deep breath. He could do that. He could tell her about his life and what he saw that life becoming now that she would be a part of it. There was just one problem. He wanted to fuck her and make her his before he did anything else. He might be as nervous as hell about turning her but he didn't feel one bit of anxiety about joining with her.

He moved to sit up and caught the blanket with his elbow. It slid down to reveal the top half of a cream-colored breast. In her effort to grab the cover El pushed it off farther, revealing the top of her other breast and one beaded nipple.

A growl rumbled up his throat and past his lips. His dick

went rock hard as need took hold and his coyote sprang to life. All thoughts of going slow fled his mind, along with the blood now flowing like boiling lava through his veins and into his cock.

He crawled up the bed and buried his face between her exposed breasts, breathing deep and filling his lungs with her scent. He brought a hand up to cup one firm mound and tweak the already hard nipple between his fingertips. Lashing with his tongue he laved the tight bud, circled it before sucking it into his mouth.

El moaned and arched into him, pushing her breasts higher for his feasting. He used his other hand to lavish attention on the breast not in his mouth, pulling at the pointed peak with gentle tugs of his fingers. With each tug his blood beat faster, hotter. Burning him from the inside out as it flowed through his body and centered in his cock.

It wasn't enough. He wanted all of her. Wanted to touch, taste and devour every inch of her. Leave no part of her unmarked by him. When he was finished, no one—least of all El—would doubt she belonged to him.

He let go of her breasts and ripped the blanket from between them, her gasp of surprise swallowed when he slammed his mouth to hers. With savage intent he took, thrust his tongue into her warm depths and plundered all he found. Teeth, tongue and lips melded in a frenzy so hot it stole his breath.

There was no time to think of gentling the kiss. El took him deeper with demands of her own. Her hands skimmed over his skin, touching everywhere they could reach. She tried to pull him down, urged him to lie on top of her. Tremors shook his arms and he dropped to his elbows, keeping his full weight off her.

Their bodies lined up, soft to hard. Hollows met ridges and

hot skin fused. Her breasts and hard nipples pressed into his chest, the peaks catching in his hair. His own nipples hardened at the contact. He ground his hips into hers, while his cock throbbed against the silky soft skin of her stomach.

Her fingernails grazed his back and sent electric shards of pleasure shooting down his spine into his balls. Heat lightning streaked to the tip of his dick where a bead of pre-cum told how close he was to exploding. Much more of this delicious torture and Brogan would disgrace himself like a randy teenager.

He pulled free of her mouth, both of them gasping for breath. Chests heaved and hearts pounded between them. If they didn't slow down it would be all over in seconds. Then again once wouldn't satisfy him and it wouldn't be long before he was ready to go again. He doubted he'd ever get enough of her.

Through hooded eyes he gazed at her swollen lips—red and puffy from his kiss—they issued an invitation to lick and nibble. But he wanted to snack on more than her mouth. He needed to feed on all of her. The slope of her neck, the arch of her shoulder, the sweep of her breast, the plane of her stomach and the valley of her sex. He planned to sample every inch of her luscious body.

He dipped his head, nibbled along her jaw and up to the soft spot below her ear. His tongue flicked out and lapped at her lobe before tracing the outer shell of her ear. El shuddered beneath him, tilted her head to give him better access to her neck. With open lips he latched on to the flesh under her ear and suckled hard, leaving his mark on her creamy skin.

Her scent and taste exploded through him, obliterating everything from his mind but El and the consuming need she dragged out of him. Need, want, desire and hunger clawed at him. His coyote urged him to take as his human side compelled him to savor. Coyote instincts pushed to the fore and his teeth lengthened.

Canines scraped but didn't break the skin on her neck as he drew his mouth down her throat to the curve beneath her chin. The flutter of her fast beating pulse vibrated on his lips. He nudged her head back with his cheek, nipped her lightly before running his tongue over the pounding hollow.

He trailed his mouth lower, headed for the breasts he'd barely spent time on. He planned to spend a lot of time on them in the future. Her skin, dewy and flushed a beautiful shade of rose, fed his need to taste. Little nips, open-mouthed kisses and sweeping licks took him to his prize. El whimpered and moaned under him, the sounds fanning the flames lashing at his reins of control.

As he moved over her plump mounds he took care to avoid the sensitive tips, heightening her arousal by teasing close, then backing away. Her hips left the bed, pushing into his and grinding his cock against her pubic bone. His balls tightened, tucked up closer to his body and pre-cum dripped from his slit.

The slick liquid coated the head and—thrusting forward— he slid his dick over her heated skin. Fire erupted, destroying the last of his control and he latched on to a taut nipple, sucked hard and thrust again and again.

El went wild, thrashing beneath him. Her orgasm took them both by surprise. Cream and heat from her pussy covered his balls. He pulled his hips back, grabbed hers in his hands and tilted her pelvis. In one hard thrust he sank into her core.

Mindless of anything but El and the hot glove surrounding his cock, he slammed into her repeatedly, rode her like the animal he was. Control and finesse long gone, he took them both on a frenzied give and take.

He pulled her legs over his hips, opened her wider, drove in deeper. His shaft hit the spot inside her slick walls that sent her crashing headfirst into another orgasm before the last one was over. Muscles with vise-like strength gripped his cock and held him tight. Buried to the hilt he had no choice but to follow her over the edge.

Fiery bursts of cum spilled from his body, took his breath with each spurt. Three, four, five times—his balls squeezed and sent his seed into the heart of El. On the last surge Brogan collapsed, managing to fall to the side and not crush her under his weight. With the little energy he had left, he wrapped his arm around her back and rolled them, his cock still buried deep inside her body.

HER TOES WERE NUMB—HER fingers too. In fact her whole body was numb and except for the fire dragging in and out of her lungs, El couldn't feel a thing. Last thing she remembered was going up in flames. Spontaneous combustion. Every time Brogan made her come it was more intense, took longer to stop and far more time to return to reality.

The man was a pleasure machine. Each stroke, every brush of his fingers or lips sent her careening into bliss. She'd never lost control the way she did with him. She didn't lose it exactly, more like handed it over for him to do whatever he wanted. Not that she would complain anytime soon. Oh no, not one word of complaint would leave her lips.

Sweat clung to her skin, tacky and warm. The moisture between her legs resembled a hot bath and Brogan's hard cock, still clamped within her pussy walls, throbbed. Little sparks of pleasure shot into her clit with each beat. Renewed arousal simmered and stirred, built in a slow, steady warmth that centered in the pit of her tummy.

Like a cat, El rubbed her face on the hard muscles of his chest. The small bud of his nipple peaked against her cheek and she turned to lick it, curled her tongue around the tip and sucked until it puckered tighter. His chest rumbled, the growl vibrating along her jaw. She gave his other nipple attention, used her fingers and nails on the one still wet from her mouth.

He stirred under her and she pinched one peak between finger and thumb while trapping the other in her teeth. Brogan bucked beneath her and his cock twitched, bumping her G-spot. Sensation burst out, making her clit pound and her pussy weep. She rotated her hips, moving up and down his erection. The pool of warmth in her belly boiled and she lifted to get more friction, deepen her lunges.

Wrapping his hands over her shoulders he pushed her up. She used her legs to lift and drop her pelvis, rolling and twisting her hips for added stimulation. Liquid flowed from her. The combination of her cream and his cum filled the air with the scent of sex.

Flesh slapped together and moans of pleasure floated around them. Their breathing grew harsh, rasped in and out as they climbed toward another peak. His fingers dug into her hips, guiding her movements, urging her to go faster. Thrusting up, he drove himself deeper on each of her down strokes.

She lost the rhythm and her balance but he held them in position, drilling her with his cock. Unrelentingly he drove them both, taking them up and over with devastating speed. Muscles lax, she fell on top of him and waited for him to stop but he continued to pump into her, building another orgasm from the ashes of the last.

A growl pierced the air. For a second she thought he'd shifted to coyote but he remained human. In a move too quick to register he changed their position until she was on her hands and knees.

Slamming forward hard, he entered her from behind. Each thrust sent him deeper and her arousal higher. With ease he had her teetering on the edge, ready to fly off. His hands cupped her breasts, his chest flush along her spine and still he powered into her. Her legs shook, from weakness or desire it didn't matter.

Being taken with a greed that bordered on savage should have been frightening, but instead of being scared she felt safe, protected, cherished. Surrounded by Brogan, she let go and gave herself over to his need. He licked her shoulder, nipped at her nape and kissed her sweat-slicked back, his mouth was as devastating to her senses as his cock.

She arched her back, pushed her hips out to take more of him. With each slide over her G-spot he pulled on her nipples and the combined sensations thrilled her, made her shake with lust. Arms braced on the headboard, she met each forward thrust. Head thrown back, she shoved backward each time he drove into her. His balls slapped her clit and she erupted.

Hot lava filled her pussy and sent her clit into spasms that bordered on pain. Every part of her electrified with the molten heat they generated. Curled over her, Brogan sank his teeth into her neck. There was no pain. The sensation at her throat was as intense as the one in her crotch and she exploded in another orgasm.

They collapsed together, legs and arms tangled. He reached for her hands, loosened her grip on the headboard and entwined their fingers. His harsh breath warmed her ear, sent tingles of delight skittering down her back. Her body lay boneless beneath him with barely the energy to breathe and yet he managed to pull desire from the depths of her soul.

He licked at her neck, little laps of his wet tongue. The spot was tender beneath his ministrations at first. With each pass the soreness lessened and El relaxed and sighed into the bedding. Brogan continued to nuzzle at her neck, calming her body and clearing her mind.

He'd bitten her.

With no warning he'd plunged his teeth into her. It hadn't hurt. If anything it had been one of the most pleasurable experiences she'd ever had. Did this mean she could shift now?

She lay still, catalogued each part of her body, tried to find any difference. Other than complete satiation she couldn't find any abnormality, any sign her body had been altered.

"El? Are you okay?" His breath puffed in her ear, fanned over her face.

"You bit me," she murmured.

"I know. I didn't mean to, it just happened. Did I hurt you?" He squeezed her fingers and rolled to his side.

"No. It didn't hurt." He snaked an arm around her stomach, pulling her back to his front, spoon fashion.

"I'm sorry. I did it on instinct. By the time I thought about it I'd already sunk my fangs into you. There was no stopping." He drew circles over her stomach with a finger.

"Am I turned now? Can I change form?" A shudder of fear at the unknown flowed through her.

"I think so, I'm not sure. I've never done this before, remember? I just know what I've been told." Pulling her hair aside, he kissed the spot where his teeth had pierced her skin.

El snuggled farther into his embrace. Her eyes grew heavy with the need for rest after their strenuous physical activity. Their heart rates had slowed, their breathing eased and cuddled against his large body she lost the will to stay awake.

9

BROGAN WATCHED El as she talked with Rowan, their heads bent close together. The serious looks on their faces told him not to interrupt. Instead he took his time to absorb every detail of his mate as she focused intently on what Rowan was saying. He knew she had questions, she'd asked him a few earlier.

When he'd woken with El in his arms, their bodies flush together and covered with the smell of sex, he'd known all was right with his world. His fear of hurting her had eased with their mating. She matched his needs with demands of her own. Life together would be a ride worth taking.

Bringing up the fact he'd neglected to use any form of protection had turned out better than he'd hoped. She'd assured him she was committed to staying and while unplanned, a pregnancy wouldn't be a bad thing. He wondered what she'd say when she found out she was already pregnant.

It didn't matter whether it was the right time to conceive or not, their mating released hormones that brought on ovulation. One more part of being turned he hadn't mentioned. He couldn't bring himself to feel guilty, the image of a very pregnant El had fused itself to his mind and he couldn't shake it. She would be beautiful full with child. His child.

He left the room with a smile that wouldn't quit and returned to his study where he waited to hear from the Council. The storm had passed hours ago and the phone lines were back on so he expected to hear from William soon. It would all depend on how quickly Marcus had informed the Council of his supposed wrongdoing.

Quinn had questioned the wisdom of waiting for the summons and suggested contacting the Council first but Brogan thought that would make him look guilty of whatever charge Marcus brought against him. The thrill of going up against his enemy raced through his veins. It had been a while since they'd bumped heads.

Heading for the window, he stared out at the snow-covered yard. Six o'clock at night and it was darker than midnight. The storm may have passed but the remaining clouds blocked out what was left of the day. He wouldn't be fronting the Council tonight. They'd have to wait for morning, if they called him in at all.

It was taking too long for them to contact him. Something was up and Brogan could only wonder what went through the mind of a man bent on getting even for an injustice that never happened. Marcus had accused him and Quinn of numerous things, the least of which being they'd stolen leadership of the pack from him.

Sovereign wasn't something one could take. It was given by the Council in accordance with the laws that governed their pack. He hadn't even wanted it at first, knew a lot of their people looked down at him because his mother was non-blood. His father might have been able to trace his lineage back to the first full-bloods to populate the area but that made no difference to those prejudiced against anyone without pure coyote parents.

"I'm worried they haven't called yet," Quinn spoke behind him.

Brogan turned to face him, leaned back on the windowsill.

"Me too. Marcus is up to something. The niggle in my gut tells me it's not going to be good. We need to be ready for anything."

"I'm worried he'll attack you this time. He wants sovereign, so getting to you would be the ultimate goal for him," Quinn reasoned.

"Well we can't do anything until the Council calls, if they call."

As if on cue, a shrill ring cut off Quinn's reply.

Brogan pushed off the window and walked the ten feet to his desk. The phone rang once more before he snatched it up.

"Hello."

"Brogan, this is William. I won't bother with the pleasantries. We'd like you and your regal to front the Council and explain some things that have been brought to our attention." Always one for getting straight to the point, William wasted no time now.

"Sure, we'll be there in the morning," he said.

"We'd like you to come into town now."

"No. The snow is still thick on the ground and I'm not risking the drive in when it's already dark. We'll be there at nine in the morning." He wouldn't budge on this. Driving in these conditions with full visibility would be bad enough. He wasn't about to do it at night.

"Fine. We'll be waiting."

The phone clicked in his ear. He placed it back on the desk and faced Quinn. "They wanted us to come in now."

"I heard. Marcus is definitely up to something if he's got

them convinced they need to see you this late." Quinn sat in the chair in front of the desk, legs stretched out.

"We knew he'd exaggerate, if not outright lie about what happened. Obviously he's spun a mighty tall yarn." Brogan skirted the desk and took his own chair. "And William asked for you to attend."

"As regal, I would be there anyway."

"Yes, but he said *you and your regal*, which for me means Marcus has concocted some tale where we're both involved." He steepled his fingers beneath his chin and thought about what William asking for the regal to attend meant.

"I guess me burying the body would have them asking to see me," Quinn conceded.

"Probably. We'll find out tomorrow."

"Was that the Council?" Rowan asked from the doorway.

"Yes, we've been summoned for tomorrow morning."

"Did they say what Marcus accused you of this time?" Rowan's frustration at Marcus and his continued campaign to have Brogan removed as sovereign rang in her voice.

"No. William didn't even mention him, just asked that my regal and I front the Council." He shrugged.

"Great. So you can't even go in there prepared. Ring them back and ask what's going on," she ordered.

Quinn chuckled and Brogan lifted an eyebrow in question.

Rowan's face flushed red but she didn't back down. "You might be sovereign, Brogan, but I'm royal and that gives me just as much right to be informed by the Council as it does for them to summon you both."

"Rowan, I know you see your position as important and it is. You're the heart of our people but when it comes to things like this the Council still functions in the old ways. Women aren't included in the management of the pack." Brogan hated to remind her of the narrow mindset of their people. He didn't much care for the reminder himself.

"Fine." She turned on her heel and left.

Brilliant. Now he had to worry about his sister's nose being out of joint.

Quinn rose from his chair. "I'll go unruffle some feathers, shall I?"

He laughed. "Yes, that would be good. I know your kind of unruffling has her in a daze for hours."

Quinn shot him a lecherous grin. "Duty calls and I must do my part as regal." He bowed low before they both burst into laughter.

With Quinn gone he finished up some paperwork. El found him as he filed the last sheets away.

"Are you busy?"

"Never too busy for you." He got up and came around the desk to meet her.

"Can we talk?"

"Sure, what's on your mind?" He hoped she wasn't upset with him over Rowan's snit.

"You turned me, right?"

He nodded.

"How do I change?"

Brogan sucked in a breath. She wanted to shift? He'd told her earlier there was no rush and she'd agreed to learn all she could before trying for the first time but she'd obviously changed her mind in the last few hours.

"Now?"

"Yes, I know I said I'd wait but I want to feel what it's like and I think it might help me to understand the new senses I've developed in the last few hours." She sniffed the air. "I didn't need to look for you with my eyes, I just followed my nose."

Ah, the increased sense of smell. Being able to smell him clearly would be a bit weird for her.

"What else have you noticed?"

"I think my vision is sharper but I'm not one hundred percent sure of that, and my hearing is better. I could hear you on the phone earlier and when you were talking with Rowan. I could have been in the room with you it was that clear."

"Those are the most prominent improvements you'll have, but there are a few others. For instance you'll have extreme sexual arousal during your time of heat." It was a shame she wouldn't be in heat for a few months, he was looking forward to the experience.

"Extreme? More than what I have been since I got here?" Her astonished tone made him laugh.

"Oh, yeah. You won't be able to go more than a couple of hours without mating." He stopped laughing when her eyes almost bugged out of her head and her mouth fell open. "It'll be fine, El. You won't ovulate like a human, it's not as frequent."

She snapped her jaw closed. "Still...*hours?*"

"Let's worry about that another time." Taking her hand he led her from the room.

"Where are we going?"

"Upstairs. You'll want the privacy of our room to shift."

"Isn't your office private enough?"

"El, you'll need to get naked to change, remember?"

She stumbled beside him and he cupped her elbow to steady her.

"Um, no. I forgot that part. I guess it wouldn't be nice for Rowan or Quinn to walk in on us."

"You'll learn that getting naked in front of other shifters is a natural and frequent thing. No one will be looking at you." He would, but that was fine since she was his to look at.

"I doubt I'll ever be able to get naked and shift in front of anyone," she mumbled under her breath.

He smiled as he led her upstairs to their room. Funny how it had changed to theirs the second he'd taken her. Whether she noticed him calling it theirs or chose to ignore it he didn't care. She'd soon learn that when coyotes mated, they shared everything.

EL FOLLOWED Brogan into his bedroom. The first thing she noticed was all her things had been moved in there. And second, he was already taking off his clothes. Staring slack-jawed, she watched the magnificent specimen he revealed inch by inch.

When he finished undressing he closed the distance between them and grabbed the hem of her shirt.

"Come on, let's get naked," he teased.

She let him strip the top over her head. When he went for the snap on her jeans she reached for his cock. Satin on steel, the hard length pulsed against her fingers. She tightened her grip, stroked down to the base and back to the head where a drop of cum beaded on the tip.

"El...keep that up and I won't be teaching you how to shift," he growled as she repeated the movement.

Smiling, she looked at him from under her lashes and used a seductive tone of voice. "Would that be so bad? We could get back to the shifting thing after we—"

She didn't get to finish. Her jeans were shoved down her legs as he put a foot on the bunched up denim and lifted her off her feet. The fabric slipped off, leaving her in her panties and socks. Not exactly a sexy look but Brogan didn't seem to care. He had her pinned to the bed with his body before she could take a breath. His mouth crushed hers as his tongue invaded and conquered any objection she might have. He stole her breath, gave her his and drew her down a path of carnal needs and wants she gladly followed him.

Their hips thrust up and down, grinding their heated flesh together. The silk barrier of her panties was no match for the fire burning between them. He reached down, grabbed the elastic edges and ripped the flimsy covering from her body.

El gasped as a growl issued from Brogan's throat. He pushed a knee between hers, shoved her legs apart to make room for his hips. His mouth ate at hers and his tongue thrust deep, laying claim to all that he touched. All thought fled when he gripped her thighs and pushed them wider and probed the slick channel at her core.

One thrust and he drove himself deep, impaling her on his throbbing flesh. His balls pulsed against her ass and the stinging hot globes branded her skin. Brogan ripped their mouths apart, dragged in a breath and stared at her from lust-filled eyes. His dilated pupils were rimmed with molten gold.

"You burn my cock with your pussy. You're so tight and hot I lose myself inside you every time."

He jerked back, slammed forward, withdrew again until the head of his cock rested at her opening.

"I want this to last forever but each time my cock touches your wet folds I'm lost in the rush." He slid in, slow and steady until pelvis met pelvis.

Matching moans of pleasure spilled past their lips. With frustrating slowness he continued to fill her over and over with deep, smooth strokes. Each lunge sent her higher but not enough to push her over the edge she frantically gripped at. Desperate nails clawed at his back, tried to urge him faster.

Lifting her legs, El curled them around his hips and dug her heels into the back of his thighs. She arched into him, used her legs to pull him down, force him deeper. Harder. Faster.

She tilted her head, her mouth grazed his neck and she bit down on the corded muscle under her lips.

He reared back, sent his cock driving into her, hitting her G-spot and clit. The results were explosive. The orgasm rolled through her, tossed her into a kaleidoscope of color and light before scattering her to the ends of the earth.

Her pussy filled with Brogan's seed. Hot bursts slashed into her as he pounded his length in and out. She licked his neck, the metallic taste of blood flowed across her tongue. Heavy lids lifted and she stared at where she'd bitten him. Shocked at her actions, she gasped. "Oh, God!"

"It's okay, El. Lick the broken skin, your saliva will help it heal," he panted.

"But..."

"Shh. I'm fine, it didn't hurt, doesn't hurt. It's what we do when we mate, a natural part of the process." Each word exploded on a puff of air as he struggled to catch his breath.

Crushed beneath Brogan's dead weight and the wound she'd inflicted staring her in the face, El fought back tears and lost. Emotions tumbled inside her, tangled up and flowed over. A sob filled her chest, shook her shoulders and slipped past her throat.

"El?" Brogan rolled them to the side. "Baby, what's wrong?" He brushed the hair from her face, the tears from her lashes.

"I...I..." She hiccupped.

"Are you hurt?"

She shook her head.

"Then what is it? Was it something I did?"

Another shake of her head.

"Baby, you're killing me here. Tell me what's wrong."

"I...bit you," she cried.

"Ah, baby, it's okay. Honest. I told you, it's normal. Please, stop crying," he pleaded.

She sniffed and buried her head into his chest. The storm of emotions receded, bringing relief from the crying she couldn't begin to explain. It wasn't just the bite. Over the last forty-eight hours so much had happened. She'd flown halfway around the world, reunited with a dear friend she'd missed terribly, almost froze to death through her own stupidity and met a man who rocked the world she lived in.

She'd made a life changing decision, one that turned her life upside down and inside out while altering her physically as well as emotionally and leaving her struggling to find her feet in a world she didn't understand. She clung to the one lifeline, the one constant, in a world that had spun out of control.

Brogan.

10

MORNING ARRIVED COLD AND SUNNY. It was just past dawn and Brogan lay awake, watching El sleep. When she'd finally settled down after her crying jag he'd gotten to the heart of the issue. There wasn't only one. There were many.

With all the things that had happened since her arrival he wasn't surprised she'd had a meltdown. She deserved one. They'd talked for hours. He'd explained some of the coyote law and things she could expect now that she was a shifter. She'd asked about his life and he'd done the same. There wasn't much left to discover about each other.

Now he had to get through this morning's meeting with the Council. Marcus had been a thorn in his side for so long Brogan wasn't sure what he'd do without him around to stir up trouble. They'd soon find out because he had every intention of this being the last time Marcus caused anyone problems.

He hated to leave the bed and El but it was past time to get up. It would take an hour by road to get into town. Over land in coyote form would be less than half that but arriving naked wouldn't be a good start to the meeting.

El didn't stir when he slipped from the bed and tucked the covers around her. Even covered, the sight of her had his libido soaring. It didn't help to have her scent all over him or the smell of sex filling the room. His cock twitched and he shook his head at the damn thing. It had a mind of its own and all it wanted was El.

It looked as if he'd be suffering through another cold shower. He swore under his breath. Cold showers and holding back his wild impulses were becoming a regular thing. Something he'd have to fix when he got the problem of Marcus out of the way.

He left the door to the bathroom open. He wanted El to know where he was if she woke to find him gone. Soap in hand, he made quick work of scrubbing down and rinsing. A squirt of shampoo later he was clean from head to toe and all the bits in between. Still sporting a semi-erection, he shut the water off and stepped out.

Peeking through the door, he saw El slept. She was curled on her side facing him and he soaked up the thrill of having her in his bed.

The towel was rough against his skin and he dragged it over his body in quick swipes, doing a rush job of drying off. Satisfied, he made his way back to the bed.

"El, baby." Hand on her shoulder, he gave her a nudge. "Come on sleepy-head, time to rise and shine."

She murmured something sounding suspiciously like a swear word and he chuckled. Not a morning person.

"Come on, El." He yanked the blanket off her. "I've got to go soon and I want to eat breakfast with you before I leave."

"Go away," she murmured as she curled up tighter.

She looked like a child. Petite as she was, the position made her look smaller, more vulnerable. He didn't like the idea of her being exposed. This afternoon he'd teach her to protect herself.

Not that she'd need to since he wasn't planning on letting her out of his sight when he returned from town.

He reached down and scooped her into his arms, her squeal of surprise delighting him.

"Time for sleeping beauty to get in the shower," he said.

"No! Coffee! Need coffee." She struggled in his grip but she was no match for his size or strength.

With one hand he turned the water on and stepped beneath the spray. She sputtered and protested but it was too late. They were both drenched.

"Jeez, Brogan," she gurgled. "If this is how you plan to wake me every morning I might re-think staying."

His arms tightened around her and bands of steel constricted his heart. She'd leave him? His heart stopped for several beats, then it took off at an alarming pace, pounding in his head and ears. Fear sliced into his soul before common sense took hold and he realized she was joking.

"You'll never leave," he breathed. "If you did I'd hunt you down and bring you back. You're mine." His final words erupted on a growl.

"What?" She turned her face to his.

"You're never leaving."

"No, I'll never leave." She placed her hands on either side of his face, pulled him closer. "I couldn't leave you if the devil himself tried to chase me away."

El kissed him. Not with the passion they'd burned with before but tenderness he'd never experienced from a woman. She poured what he hoped was her soul into that one locking of lips. Gently, he plied her mouth open, dipped inside and handed over everything he was in return.

BY THE TIME they made it out of the shower, Brogan had ten

minutes to gulp down the bacon and eggs Rowan had made. At the dining table they rarely used, he talked with Quinn about the meeting and reminded both Rowan and El to stay inside. His gut was telling him not to leave the house but as sovereign he had no choice. He pushed back from the table and picked up his plate.

"Leave that. You and Quinn get going. The quicker you get there the quicker you can sort it out and come home," Rowan said.

"Okay." He put the plate back down. "Remember what I said. We have no idea what Marcus is up to so don't leave the house, not even to go on the front steps." He threw El a pointed look. "Either of you."

He headed for the door, his mind already switching gears to what lay ahead.

"Ahem," Rowan cleared her throat in an exaggerated fashion. "Aren't you forgetting something, Quinn?"

Brogan stopped and turned to see what his sister was talking about. Quinn, who'd been a step behind him, hightailed it across the room to Rowan and bent over to kiss her goodbye. With a sheepish grin on his face, he apologized before scuttling back to Brogan.

Because El hadn't made a point of asking or even commenting, he made sure she knew how much he'd miss her while he was gone. Striding over, he pulled her from her seat and plastered his mouth to hers. When he came up for air they were both breathless and her eyes held that dreamy look he was coming to love.

The trouble was he now sported a hard-on in his jeans. Good thing they had an hour before they hit Whispering Springs.

• • •

BROGAN'S HANDS were wrapped around the leather steering wheel in a white-knuckled grip. The mountain road was treacherous at the best of times but after a snowfall it turned deadly. With care, he kept the speed as fast as possible without risking losing control on the slippery surface. Each mile he put between him and El made his gut tighten.

It was more than the need to be with his mate. All his coyote instincts were screaming and his beast pulled at its restraints. The hair on his nape stood on end, his heart pounded as if he'd run ten miles and his palms, slick with sweat, slid on the wheel. Disaster loomed up ahead but what it could be eluded him.

On the approach to town the road was littered with branches and snowdrifts from the plows that would have been through first thing this morning. No large trees had fallen that he'd seen and he hoped the destruction was minimal everywhere. Some pack members had suffered considerable damage in the last blizzard but he didn't think yesterday's had been as bad.

They hit the end of Spring Road and were brought to a standstill. Traffic backed up the whole length as far as the eye could see. Four-wheel drives lined the street bumper to bumper. More off-road vehicles filled the parking spots along the side. Either everyone in Whispering Springs had come to town for supplies to make repairs or word had spread about the sovereign being summoned.

Quinn whistled low, the sound piercing in the cab of the truck. "Looks like we've got an audience."

"It'll take hours to drive through this lot." Making a snap decision, Brogan spun the wheel and made a u-turn. He turned onto School Road and parked in front of the two-story high school building.

"I guess we're walking," Quinn said as he undid his seatbelt and opened the door.

"Yep, we'll get there a hell of a lot faster. Besides, being seen in the open will give the impression I've got nothing to hide, which I don't." Brogan got out and walked around the hood to the curb. He pushed the lock button on his key as he met Quinn on the path.

The rumble of a diesel engine vibrated the ground beneath their feet. Pivoting, he saw Steven McKenna pull the town's big snow plow onto the street. Huge wheels rolled over tarmac and brought the machine closer. Steve had the plow scoop up, there was no snow on the road now. The main streets would have been plowed first thing and there hadn't been a drop of snow since the evening before.

Parking behind Brogan's truck, the big engine rattled and shook the hunk of metal in its final breath of life as Steve cut the power. The scent of diesel hung heavy in the air, coating Brogan's nose and throat.

Steve flung the heavy door open and jumped down from the cab.

"Hey, Brogan, Quinn." Steve nodded at them as he strode around to where they waited on the footpath. He slapped Brogan on the back in greeting. "So I hear you're forcing humans to turn now."

About to take a step, Brogan faltered and turned to look at his friend and fellow shifter with his mouth hanging open.

"Well, now we know what kind of shit Marcus is spreading," Quinn said.

Steve's smile spread from ear to ear. "And don't forget he's going around killing off the naturals in some underhanded attempt to rule the coyote world." Steve laughed.

Brogan didn't see the funny side. "What other venom is he spewing?"

"What? That's not enough?" Steve continued to chuckle. "He claims to have seen you attack a natural to impress some human woman who you then forced to turn into a shifter. Just the usual bullshit that spills every time Marcus opens his mouth."

"You obviously aren't buying into it. What's the rest of the pack saying?" Quinn asked.

Steve was the closest thing to a gossip columnist the pack had. He outdid the old biddies with his knowledge of what went on in and around Whispering Springs. If anyone could get Brogan the information he needed, it was Steve.

"Most are inclined to think it's bullshit but it's the human in the equation that has everyone curious. The entire pack knows a human arrived at your place the other day." Steve aimed a questioning look at Brogan.

Brogan knew his friend didn't really think he'd force the change on El. His interest was more in El herself. It wasn't often a human came through town, never mind a single female. A bolt of jealousy and possessiveness speared his gut.

"Mine," he growled, the beast rearing its head in defense of its mate.

Hands up, Steve took a step back. "Whoa! Stand down, Brogan. I'm not planning on poaching."

He shook himself, tried to remember this was his childhood friend who would never stab him in the back.

"Sorry. I'm still coming to grips with everything."

"No worries. So you found your mate then." It was a statement, not a question.

"Yes, El's the woman Rowan lived with in Australia for all those years. She's here for the wedding."

Quinn laughed. "And she'll be staying for one of her own."

Steve stuck out his hand. "Congratulations! For what it's worth, I think this may cement your standing as sovereign.

Producing the next generation will put you in good stead with the Council."

Brogan shook the offered hand. "Thanks. After this latest Marcus-emitted bullshit is cleared up why don't you come out to the house and meet her?"

"I'd love to, but I've got a date." Steve waggled his eyebrows.

"Anyone we know?" Quinn asked.

"Nah, she's from the city, visiting over in Mountain Pass. Friend of a friend kind of thing." He shrugged. "Doubt anything will come of it. Come on, let's get to this shindig and see what happens."

They headed in the direction of Spring Street. Brogan nodded hello to those they passed. He even stopped to talk to a few but he tried to make the stops short. That niggling sensation in his gut was getting bigger. It was more like a nudge now. Two blocks from the community center he remembered what he'd wanted to ask Steve.

"Hey, Steve, do you know what Marcus is up to? Other than spreading garbage around."

"Nothing I would consider unusual. I know he's been in town less and less over the last few weeks. Could be the weather, though. We've had some mean storms rolling in recently." Steve turned to look at him. "Why? Got something you want me to look at?"

"No. Nothing I can put a finger on. Just keep your eyes and ears open for me."

"Sure. If I see or hear anything, I'll let you know."

No one spoke again until they reached the community center where Steve bade them farewell to go get himself some breakfast at The Den Café. Brogan and Quinn made their way to the closed-door meeting and the Council members waiting for them.

11

EL CAME DOWNSTAIRS after taking up Brogan's clean laundry. Not even one day as his mate and already waiting on him hand and foot. Shaking her head, she smiled. She wasn't really waiting on him but helping Rowan out. After they'd cleared away the breakfast dishes Rowan had started in on the dirty clothes.

El had never seen a mountain of laundry before. The pile started on the floor and stood higher than her waist. Load after load went from washer to dryer. The process took half the morning but there was finally nothing left to wash. Just pile after pile of folded clothes to be put away.

Rowan was upstairs still and El decided to get a start on dinner. She could throw a pot of spaghetti sauce on to simmer and then they'd just have to put the pasta in to boil when they were ready to eat. It also freed up the rest of the day for her and Rowan to talk. Brogan hadn't been much help with learning to shift. His less than helpful instructions were "Just think about your inner coyote and it'll happen."

How was she supposed to think of her inner coyote when

she'd never had one? He'd promised to help her later but she wanted to try before he got home. If she could manage the change with Rowan's help she could surprise him when he got here and maybe they could go for a run in the woods. The idea of running wild in the forest with Brogan at her side sent a shiver down her spine and warmth through her chest.

Another question she wanted to ask Rowan was whether or not they mated in coyote form. El wasn't sure she was ready for that if they did, but she needed to know everything about living as a shapeshifter. Brogan had said her cycle would be different too. Did that mean pregnancy would also be different?

Oh God. Would she give birth to a pup? Or worse! A litter of puppies?

Shuddering at the mental image, she searched the pantry for ingredients. Her great grandmother's sauce recipe had been passed down through the females of her family, like a rite of passage.

Rowan burst through the door. "Hey, what are you doing?"

"Making spaghetti sauce for dinner."

"Grandma's sauce?" Rowan licked her lips.

"Yep."

"Oh God." She dropped on a stool at the island counter. "I haven't indulged in that particular brand of heaven since I left Australia."

"I promise to make enough for you to freeze some for another night." El laughed. Every time she made enough for more than one meal, Rowan managed to empty the saucepan, even going as far as trying to lick the bottom of the pot.

"You won't have to. Now that you're mated with Brogan you can make it fresh for me whenever I want it." Rowan sat with a smug look on her face.

"I should teach you to make it yourself," El said, knowing it would never happen. They'd shared a house for nearly three years and she hadn't managed it.

"That would spoil the 'handed-down-through-the-family' feel to it."

Rowan was right. It wouldn't be the same without a Crawford woman stirring the pot.

"Can I ask you something, El?"

"Sure."

"Did Brogan turn you?"

Her gaze jerked up to meet Rowan's. "Why?"

"Well, there's a change in your scent that you might not be aware of."

"What sort of change?"

"Um, I'm not sure I should be the one telling you this. Just answer my question. Did Brogan turn you?"

"Yes."

"Did he explain what happens when a female human is turned?"

"About the increased sex drive when I'm in heat?"

"No. Well, yes, there is that, but there's something else I'm sure my brother conveniently forgot to tell you." Rowan chewed her lip.

"What? We talked last night about a lot of things so maybe he did tell me."

"When a female human is turned during mating, the hormones and chemicals released into her system by the act of joining and by the bite increase the chances of getting pregnant."

"Oh, that's okay. We talked about an unplanned pregnancy. It's not the right time of the month for me, Rowan so I'm not worried about it. And truthfully if it happened I wouldn't be upset."

"Maybe I didn't say that right. El, the chance of you getting pregnant is very high. As I said the hormones released push your system, kind of prodding it so that you are ready to conceive," Rowan explained.

"Okay." El wasn't worried about getting pregnant. It was extremely unlikely, she was at the very beginning of her cycle and she'd always been as regular as clockwork.

"El?"

Rowan waited until she looked up.

"What?"

"You're pregnant."

El burst out laughing. She couldn't be pregnant. Well, she could but it wasn't likely and even if she was, a doctor couldn't tell yet. God, an egg wouldn't have even made it to her uterus yet.

When Rowan didn't laugh and there was no hint of a smile on her lips, El sobered. "But..."

"What Brogan forgot to mention, and I've botched up completely explaining, is the act of turning a human female forces her system into overdrive and stimulates her ovaries making them produce eggs. I've never known any woman who hasn't conceived when being turned."

Rowan got up, came around the island and wrapped her arm around El's shoulders.

"Last night your scent was different but I put it down to mating with Brogan. This morning when you came down for breakfast I thought I could smell the change again. After spending all morning together I know what I smell, you're definitely pregnant."

"Pregnant?" El's hand covered her lower stomach. Surely she would know if she'd conceived a child? Wouldn't she feel it?

"I didn't tell you when you first got here because we've kept it just between Quinn, me and Brogan but I'm two months pregnant. I haven't been to town in all that time because the minute I step out on one of those streets the whole shifter community will know. We want to wait until after the wedding to tell people."

El absorbed what Rowan said. Inside both of them grew new life. Their children would be almost the same age. They could grow up together. Cousins. A little numb from what she'd learned, she still couldn't stop the thrill that started to grow inside her heart.

She'd grow up an only child of only children and her parents had been older so El had lost them both early. Both had died within weeks of each other when El was twenty.

The idea of being part of a family again. Of her child having a cousin to play with on a daily basis sent a surge of pleasure through her. She'd be experiencing all the joys of having her first child with her best friend. It was mindboggling.

"I should say congratulations," El uttered.

A child.

Brogan's child.

"El, you're looking a bit pale, maybe we should sit down for a minute." Rowan's concern touched a soft spot in El and tears sprang to her eyes.

She reached her arms around her best friend, pulling her close for a hug. Rowan hugged her back and they stood in the bright kitchen and cried. Not sad tears but happy, emotional tears.

When they stopped, they both dried their eyes and finished putting the ingredients for the sauce together in silence, each lost in thought. After mulling over everything, El was more determined to learn how to shift before Brogan got home. She wanted to surprise him with both the ability to change and her pregnancy.

He probably already knew she was pregnant but she wanted to tell him. And then she wanted to show him.

"Teach me to shift."

"What?"

"I haven't changed yet and Brogan wasn't very helpful when I asked him how to do it. I want to be able to shift before he comes home. I want to surprise him and I'm sure he already knows he got me pregnant."

Rowan smiled. "Oh, yeah, he'd know."

"So will you help me?"

"Of course. Let's get this all cleared away and we can get started."

Together they put the last of the ingredients into the pan and put it on to simmer. They cleared away the garbage and stacked the dirty dishes in the dishwasher. When the last counter was wiped and the kitchen was filled with the smell of tomato and spices, they made their way into the lounge room to discuss the fine art of shifting.

"Brogan said he thinks about his inner coyote and he shifts but I've never had a coyote so how can I think of it?"

"Until I came home last year, I hadn't shifted since before I left. I couldn't remember what my coyote looked like so I just pictured Quinn and Brogan. It might be harder for you. I've only ever been with one turned human for their first time and that was over ten years ago. But Gordie grew up in the pack so that wouldn't really help anyway."

Rowan walked over to the fireplace, picked up a couple of photo frames and made her way back to El.

"Here, if we put these pictures of Brogan in front of you they might help. Sit on the floor next to the coffee table, that way you won't have to drop down as you change."

"Should I take my clothes off?" El asked.

"Oh yeah, sorry. Do you want me to close the curtains?"

"Would you mind?" El wasn't concerned with Rowan seeing her naked but didn't want to give anyone else coming around a free show.

Going to each of the windows, Rowan pulled the curtains closed. Returning to El, she began removing her clothes.

"Why are you taking your clothes off?"

"I thought you might be more comfortable if we did it together. It might help you to shift if I'm doing it too," Rowan said.

"Thank you," El choked out. Her eyes stung with the emotions bubbling inside her. "Sorry, I'm turning into an emotional wreck."

Laughing, Rowan said, "Get used to it. I cry at the drop of a leaf these days. Everything I've read about being pregnant says it's normal and part of the joy of carrying a new life."

"I can't believe the things I've done since getting here. There's been a whole load of firsts for me in the last few days," El sniffled.

"You don't regret coming, do you?"

They were both naked now.

"No. I don't regret anything, least of all coming to see you."

Rowan sat on the floor and El followed. Sitting next to each other with the photos of Brogan in coyote form in front of them, El looked at the beautiful animal and tried to picture herself as one. Her muscles stretched, pulled and her skin tightened but nothing else happened. She closed her eyes and concentrated.

She pulled her bottom lip between her teeth and bit into the soft flesh. The sharp sting sucked the breath from her lungs as she gasped in pain.

"What? Are you all right?" Rowan asked.

Rowan gasped when El opened her mouth to answer.

"Your teeth have changed and I think you've bitten your

lip," she said. Reaching over with a tissue she'd grabbed from the table, Rowan dabbed gently on the wound.

El ran her tongue over canine teeth, the long sharp fangs strange to touch. A wicked grin split her mouth.

"I did it! I changed!"

"Not quite." Rowan chuckled.

"Well sure, but it's a start. Don't take my victory from me." She pouted.

"Okay, let's try again. Did you feel anything else changing?"

"Yes, my muscles and skin pulled tight first and then my teeth changed."

"Your eyes have changed color too. They're not as light. The blue has gone a couple of shades darker."

"Really? I want to see them, but I want to try again first."

She closed her eyes, thought about the changes she'd managed so far and the next thing she knew she was looking at things from a different angle. The smell of the room filled her nose and made her sneeze. She sniffed the air. A bark next to her had her turning to Rowan.

Damn!

They'd done it. Rowan's coyote form wasn't as big as Brogan's and her coloring not as light, she had white mixed in with dark gray. Looking down at her paws, El tried to decide if she liked the color of her coat.

Rowan's ears twitched and she looked toward the door. El titled her head, tried to hear what had drawn her friend's attention. It took less than a second for Rowan to shift back to human.

"Change back, El," she commanded as she dragged her clothes on. "Quick, change back. Get dressed."

Panic seized her. She sat frozen in coyote form as Rowan pulled the last of her clothes on and ran from the room. Shattering glass and timber echoed through the house and El stood on two legs in human form without knowing how she'd done it. Scrabbling into her clothes she heard Rowan scream and footsteps pounded down the hall.

She'd just gotten her sweater on when a man dressed in black burst into the room and charged toward her. The scream caught in her throat as he tackled her to the floor. She kicked out, tried to free herself from his grasp but he pinned her to the ground with his weight. He outweighed her by at least a hundred pounds.

His forearm pressed into her throat, cutting off her air. Clawing at his arm with her hands, she couldn't get a hold of the slick, skin-like black clothing. Her heart pounded in her ears, her lungs burned with the need for air and stars exploded across her vision. The last thing El heard before everything went black was his malicious laughter.

12

BROGAN PACED THE MEETING ROOM. The seven other members of the pack sat in silence. No one had spoken a word since he and Quinn had arrived. William was the one to break the quiet.

"There's no point getting agitated, Sovereign. Marcus should be here soon."

Brogan glared at him without breaking stride. Every instinct he had screamed at him to return to El. Something wasn't right. Marcus took every opportunity to undermine his leadership with the eagerness of a teenager getting his first taste of pussy. So where the hell was he?

Something was definitely wrong.

"Five more minutes and we're leaving," he growled.

He had to get back to El. He'd left her at the house with Rowan. She should be safe and the time together would be good for El, she could learn a lot from his sister but he wanted to be close by. Needed to be close to her.

There was a ruckus outside the room before the door crashed open. Expecting Marcus to have arrived Brogan turned to find Rowan, red-faced and covered in sweat. Naked as the day she was born, Rowan stood, her chest heaving for breath. Steve slipped into the room behind her.

Quinn was out of his chair, stripping off his jacket and across the room in a second. Like a gunshot, the echo of his chair hitting the floor thundered in the quiet room.

"He took her!" Rowan gasped out.

Every muscle went taut. Every nerve sprang to life and Brogan's coyote fought to be free.

"What the hell?" Quinn struggled to get Rowan covered. "Let me get my jacket on you."

"No. He took her," she repeated taking a step toward Brogan.

"When?" He didn't need to ask who, it was obvious by his conspicuous absence at this meeting he'd prompted.

Marcus.

I'll kill him!

"I don't know how long." Rowan's breathing had eased and Quinn lowered her into a chair William pulled over.

"Oh my God! You're hurt!" Quinn pulled her from the seat, took her place and cradled Rowan in his lap. "You're bleeding, Rowan." Color drained from Quinn's face.

Brogan strode over, pushed William out of the way to get to his sister. "What the hell happened, Rowan? Who hurt you?"

"It's okay." Her words were laced with exhaustion. "Just a bump."

"Like fuck it's 'just a bump.' The damn thing is bleeding down your back." Quinn's barely suppressed anger vibrated in his voice.

Brogan lifted the hair from the back of Rowan's neck and saw the trail of red running from her scalp. Examining the cut on the back of her head, he decided she'd probably need stitches.

"Get Doc," Brogan barked.

One of the Council members scuttled off to do his bidding and he turned Rowan's head gently to look at her eyes.

"How long were you out, Rowan?"

"Don't know," she murmured.

"Do you know where he took El?" Fear for El clawed at his gut and gave him a harsh tone.

"No, I lost them. They were gone when I came to. I followed their scent through the woods but he had a vehicle waiting about halfway down the drive. I just know he took the road north. He went up the mountain, not down." Her words were starting to slur and her eyelids drooped then finally closed as she used the last of her energy.

The room around them came to life with the councilmen talking over one another. Doc Munroe hustled in closely followed by two guys pushing a gurney.

"Lay her on the bed, Quinn," Gordie Munroe ordered.

Indecision flashed in Quinn's eyes. Brogan knew he'd be torn between getting Rowan the care she needed and not wanting to let her go. Brogan could relate. He'd felt the same when El had been caught in the snowstorm.

Steve stepped close beside him. "Brogan, I think I know where he's gone." He kept his voice low so only Brogan would hear.

"Where?"

"I overheard some of the old-timers at the Café. They were talking about Marcus and something he'd said. It rang some bells and with what Rowan just said about him going up the mountain, I think he's taking her to the canyon. He's luring you there."

Rowan moaned as Doc probed her head wound, diverting Brogan's attention for a minute. Moving to her side, he stood next to Quinn and waited to hear what Gordie found.

"How far along is she?" Gordie asked.

"Two months." He and Quinn spoke together.

Gordie looked at them and smiled. "I don't think there's anything to worry about but I want to do an MRI of her head and an ultrasound for the baby just to be sure. We need to get her over to the clinic."

"Go with her, Quinn. I'll take Steve and go after El," Brogan said.

Rowan's hand shot out and grabbed his forearm. Her nails, not yet fully retracted from coyote form, dug into his flesh.

"No, take Quinn. He's the best tracker in the pack." Her eyes pleaded with him. "Bring her back."

"Rowan—" Brogan began.

"Don't you dare treat me like a delicate female. I just ran all the way from the house after being bashed over the head. I think I can manage to get a couple of scans done. Gordie knows what she's doing. I couldn't be in better hands."

"She's right. We need Quinn to get us close without being heard and there are no better hands than Gordie's." Steve directed a challenging look at Gordie and she visibly bristled.

"Please, Brogan," Rowan begged.

"Brogan, we need to go get your mate now, we have no idea how long he's had her or what he's got planned," Steve said.

He squeezed his eyes closed, tried to think beyond the need to get his mate and act like sovereign. Rowan was right, she was in the best hands and they did need Quinn to find El. Opening his eyes, he looked at his regal.

"I won't pull rank, it's up to you but I will say she's right. You are the best tracker we have. Doc is more than capable of looking after Rowan and the baby until we get back and it's unlikely Marcus will try anything in town. I doubt he'd even show his face now that he's snatched El."

"Rowan, honey, are you sure?" Quinn leaned in close, brushed his lips over Rowan's.

"Yes. Go get her and this time he doesn't get away with it, Quinn."

Brogan didn't think there was any worry on that score. Marcus had finally done something he couldn't cover up. He turned to face William.

"Marcus will be exiled from the pack if he makes it out alive." As sovereign he could decree the removal of a member with the support of the Council and he had no doubt they would support him on this one.

No coyote messed with another's mate, least of all the sovereign's.

THE FIRST THING El noticed was the pain lancing her side. She was lying on hard ground, sharp jagged edges digging through her clothes into her ribs and hipbone. The second thing she reacted to was the cold. She shivered as her senses came more awake. Moaning, she tried to move her legs and couldn't. Something held them together.

Her eyes popped open, her vision unfocused at first but as it cleared she took note of her surroundings. She also took note of the fact her ankles and wrists were tied together with rope. The quiet indicated no one was near and remaining perfectly still, she concentrated on listening for any clue she wasn't alone.

Nothing.

Not even the raspy sound of breathing.

She had no idea where he'd taken her or where he'd gone. The ground around her had been cleared of snow, small mounds of white sat in front of her and it covered all the trees and shrubs in sight. A rock or stick dug into her thigh as she twisted to look behind her. The view was the same. He'd left her outside, in the forest somewhere.

Urgency grabbed hold. She needed to get away before whoever had taken her came back. El had no idea who the man was or what he wanted but the thought of him returning sent ice rushing through her veins and fear exploding in her gut. If he'd left her here, he'd meant for her to die alone. If not, he planned to come back. El didn't like either of those ideas.

Clouds covered the sky, blocking out the sun so she couldn't make out what time it was or which direction he'd taken her. The freezing temperature made her numb, but the rope around her limbs added to the sensation by cutting off her circulation. She wouldn't be able to get away with her hands and feet tied. How could she get free? The nylon cords were biting into her flesh and she hadn't tried to loosen them yet.

She needed to think, clear her mind of the panic and fear then work out a way to get untied and back to Rowan. El didn't know what had happened at the house but she was pretty sure the guy who'd taken her had hurt her friend. Had Brogan and Quinn come back from their meeting and found Rowan hurt and El missing? Were they out here looking for her?

Pain streaked up her arms and pulling them in front of her for a closer look took effort. Biting her lip to stop from crying out, El studied the knots at her wrists. It didn't look as if she'd be able to undo them. Her abductor hadn't been kind enough to leave her with a neat bow to loosen them. She pulled the ropes to her mouth and used her teeth to tug at dirt-covered fibers.

They didn't give and the movement rubbed the raw skin already circling both her arms. She needed something sharp. There was no hope of getting through the thick rope with her teeth. Frustration bubbled and a growl slid up her throat. Muscle and skin stretched and her teeth lengthened.

Her teeth.

With renewed hope, she brought her hands to her mouth and sank her coyote teeth into the knots. El gnawed at the ropes, felt them give a little. She could do this. Wiggling her hands and fingers to bring back the circulation, she bit down harder. One strand snapped, fell from her wrist. It gave her room to move and soon a second and third piece of rope fell away.

El breathed through the pain as blood surged back into her fingers. She shook her hands, clenched and unclenched her fists to try and ease the throb. She gritted her teeth and used her stiff arms to push herself up. The agony in her ribs eased but there would be bruises. The dull ache was manageable and she didn't appear to have suffered any other injuries. Her legs, numb and weak from lack of blood, hurt but she drew them up to examine her ankle restraints.

She was greeted with bigger and more complicated knots than the ones on her wrists. She growled and bent double, thanking her lucky stars for years of gymnastics and yoga. Flexibility had always been her strong point. Her back and shoulders ached as she stretched to reach the knots with her teeth. Sensing victory within her grasp, El ripped at the ropes with teeth as sharp as a knife.

The last tie gave way and slipped to the ground and El checked her sore, bleeding ankles. The abrasions were covered in dirt but there was no time to tend them. She scanned the area and saw no sign of her attacker. Sniffing the air, she could only pick up a faint trace of him. There hadn't been time to take note of him when he'd grabbed her at the house but one thing she did know from his scent, he was a coyote shifter.

What he hoped to gain by bringing her out here and leaving her she couldn't guess but she would not let him win. Logic told her the man Brogan had told her about was behind this. Whether he'd been the one to take her or someone else it didn't matter, she'd fight for everything she cared about. Rowan, Brogan and the baby she carried inside. She wouldn't let Marcus take what she'd only just discovered. Whatever his game, she'd do all she could to get back to the house and Rowan.

Or had he left Rowan out here too? Was she bound somewhere nearby?

El struggled to her feet and her knees wobbled before holding firm. On shaky legs, she turned to check for any sign of life. She couldn't smell anyone else. Felt sure she was out here on her own. There was no trace of Rowan.

The only sign of life was a set of footprints in the snow leading away through the trees. Drawing in a deep breath, El took a tentative step, her stride shaky at first but with each tread her legs grew steadier and she followed the trail in the hope of finding her way out of the forest.

With each footstep El knew she was in trouble. Bare feet and snow didn't mix. She'd been taken without a coat and her jeans and sweater weren't enough to keep the cold from sinking all the way down to her bones, their dampness wasn't helping either. Gingerly she walked through the slush, her toes growing colder by the second. Numbness moved up from her feet and dulled the pain of her abused ankles but that was little comfort when she found herself lost in the middle of an unknown forest for the second time in as many days.

Her best option was to shift. She'd only managed the complete change once but if she wanted to survive she had no choice. Taking coyote form would give her a few important advantages, the best one being her attacker didn't know she could shift.

El stripped out of her clothes and buried them under a snow drift. No point leaving clues. Her first attempt gave her claws, teeth and a coating of fur. Shivering she tried again but with her body racked by cold she found it hard to concentrate. Sucking in a deep breath she gave the last of her energy to shifting.

This time she slid into it with ease. A pleased rumble filled her chest but she knew not to let it out. She needed to be silent. Using her heightened sense of smell, she followed the trail of human prints, listening for signs she was close to another form of life. Moving off to the side of the tracks, she walked slowly, padding lightly through the snow to make as little noise as possible.

The trail weaved its way through the forest and she was starting to wonder if he was walking in circles to confuse anyone that might follow. Who, other than her, might want to track her kidnapper was easy to work out. If Brogan had discovered her abduction he'd be out looking for her, she knew to the depth of her soul that he'd search until he found her and the man responsible for attacking her.

She hoped the man had left some sort of clue as to where he'd taken her or Brogan could search the Whispering Mountains for days and not find her. Not that she was going to wait around to be rescued. The thought of sitting in the cold snow didn't appeal even if she was the type to expect someone else to solve her problems.

With renewed determination, El continued to move forward, being careful to listen and smell for any danger that may be lurking nearby. The forest was quiet around her and it felt like she was the only person alive in the whole world. If the situation wasn't so deadly it would be beautiful. She was quickly learning that looks could be very deceiving. Just look at what she'd become. A mythical creature she'd only ever dreamed of before now.

A shapeshifter.

13

BROGAN TOSSED his phone onto the dashboard.

"Who was that?" Steve asked.

"Doc. She said Rowan and the baby are fine. And she wanted to let me know that word of El's abduction has spread. More than half the town is moving out into the mountainside to help search for her and Marcus."

"It might be better if someone else finds him." Quinn's quiet words sent chills down Brogan's spine. He knew his friend wanted to kill Marcus with his bare hands for hurting Rowan. Hell, he felt the same way.

"We'll find him. And Steve, you're our safety net. You'll be the one to take him down."

Steve chuckled wryly. "What makes you think I don't want to kill him as much as you two?"

"Your devotion to our friendship is admirable," Brogan said.

"It has nothing to do with our friendship. I promised not to say anything and I won't but I can tell you he's done some damage to a mutual friend that should have gotten him exiled months ago." Steve's cryptic words had Brogan seething.

Quinn growled beside him. "Does this have to do with Doc?"

"You know?" Steve's astonishment was clear.

"No. All I know is Rowan helped her and refused to tell me what went on," Quinn clarified.

"I want to know the full story when we get back to town," Brogan demanded.

"She won't tell you. She doesn't want anyone to know. Ever," Steve said.

Whispering Mountain lookout was around the next bend and the four-wheel drive parked on the side of the road proved Steve's hunch right. Pulling in behind they jumped from Brogan's truck, Steve and Quinn each heading to a different corner of Marcus's vehicle to deflate the tires. The bastard would not be getting away by car if he managed to elude them.

Tinted windows made seeing inside difficult but there were no bulky shadows big enough to be El. Besides, Marcus might be an idiot but he wouldn't leave her in the car and go off. No, he'd take her into the forest and make sure she couldn't get away.

Quinn finished disabling the car and stood. Scanning the area, he moved off the embankment and into the tree line, tracking their prey. Brogan and Steve moved in behind, letting Quinn lead the way through the trees. They'd trekked for about ten minutes when Quinn stopped abruptly. He took a deep breath and analyzed the air.

"Marcus isn't far ahead of us, his scent is stronger." Quinn turned and sniffed again. "There's another coyote near."

A dark blur of motion drew Brogan's attention to the left. A coyote he'd never seen before pounced on him, taking his legs out from under him and knocking the wind from his lungs as they crashed to the ground together. He struggled to keep the sharp teeth and powerful jaws from closing over his throat.

He lost his grip on the damp fur and the coyote lunged for his head. Braced for the pain of teeth piercing skin, he was shocked when the animal licked his face from jawbone to forehead. The second swipe finished in his ear, drool leaving a sticky trail.

Fingers twined in the fur around the animal's neck, Brogan held the beast still and stared into a pair of eyes he knew well. Seeing the familiar gaze coming from a coyote stunned him.

"Shit! *El?*"

Her exuberant barks made him laugh. Jeez, she'd shifted. He pushed her off, wanting to get to his feet and look at all of her. A snarl had them all turning. Not fifteen feet away stood Marcus in coyote form and before any of them could react, the animal sprang forward.

In human form, Brogan would sustain a lot of damage before getting the upper hand against a coyote as large as Marcus but his enemy never got the chance to hurt him. With a bark so fierce at first he hadn't thought it came from her, El attacked. She plowed into Marcus's side, taking him to the ground.

Her agility and fast movement surprised all of them. She had the other coyote pinned to the snow, her razor sharp teeth poised around its vulnerable neck. One bite and it would all be over.

He couldn't let her do that.

Marcus whined and his eyes bulged. Brogan knew she'd broken skin.

"El, let him go. We won't let him get away but you have to let go." He inched closer to where they were, Quinn coming around the other side. "Eloise, you don't want to do this," he coaxed. "Come on, let him go. Quinn and Steve will make sure he doesn't get away. He'll answer to the Council for what he's done and be exiled from the pack."

She didn't move, frozen in place with Marcus quivering beneath her. In coyote form her every instinct would be screaming to finish off the other animal, eliminate the threat.

Quinn moved into her line of sight and she growled a low warning in her throat. Marcus flinched and whimpered.

"El, please, baby. For me, let him go," Brogan pleaded. He'd get down on his knees and beg if he had to. If she killed Marcus she'd have to live with the guilt. He didn't wish that on her no matter how much he wanted Marcus dead.

She finally let go of Marcus' throat but didn't get off him. El held him down with bared teeth and her weight. After Quinn got him by the scruff she got up, trotted to Brogan and sat on her haunches like a domesticated pet instead of the wild coyote she'd just been.

He reached down, ran his fingers through her gray coat. She was damp and cold. For the second day she'd been caught out in the snow. He hoped this wouldn't become a habit.

"You can change back now, El."

Quinn coughed, cleared his throat. "That might not be such a good idea."

"Why not? I want to check she's okay, that he didn't hurt her," Brogan argued.

"Brogan," Steve interjected. "As much as I'm a guy and getting a look at a naked woman is one of my constant aims in life, I don't think she'd be comfortable being naked in front of us."

"Oh, right. I guess I'm so used to that part I just don't think about it." He was never this thoughtless. She scrambled his brains so much he was forgetting the basics. "But she can't go to town in coyote form."

"You've got a blanket in your truck don't you?" Steve asked. "She can shift back and wrap it around her. She needs to see Doc."

"We'll wait here, give you a head start so she can change without an audience," Quinn added.

Brogan looked at his two friends, thought about warning them against doing anything to Marcus but decided not to. He trusted them to bring him back safely to face the Council.

"Come on, El, let's go to the truck."

She padded along beside him, comfortable in her coyote form. She was a beautiful animal. Her coat, though damp, looked healthy and the colors were a mixture of different shades of gray. A little gold around the ears and neck gave her a warm glow. She was an average size and considering how small she was in human form, Brogan found that strange.

It wouldn't matter what she looked like, he'd still want her. His coyote clawed to be let free. He wanted to run through the forest with her by his side, but that pleasure would wait for later. First they had to get her to Doc's clinic.

And Marcus back to town.

WITH MARCUS RESTRAINED in the back of Brogan's truck, the drive down the mountain was made in silence. El was too exhausted to talk and lay quietly in Brogan's arms while Quinn drove and Steve rode up front. The men had been very careful not to crowd her when they'd emerged from the woods. No one would look her in the eye and they let Brogan bundle her into the back without comment.

El had kept her gaze away from Marcus. While she didn't fear him, knew after their little wrestle she could take him if she had to, she didn't want to look at the coyote who threatened to take so much from them all. Brogan had told her Rowan was injured but okay and he continued to reassure her that everything would be fine now, but the reality of what she'd been through was beginning to sink in.

Her own injuries were minor but she would see the doctor just to be sure. The warmth seeping into her from Brogan lulled her to a light doze and she snuggled closer. With her arms wrapped around his neck, El held on, not wanting to let go of him ever again.

Jolted from sleep, El grabbed Brogan tighter. Silence reigned for a second before pandemonium broke free. People called out, their voices muffled by the car until Quinn opened his door and the noise became a roar. Faces crowded against the windows, staring in at her and El shrank back into Brogan.

"Get them away from the truck," Brogan bellowed.

Steve jumped from the cab, pushing bodies away from the vehicle as he did. Quinn came around to the curb and opened the door, reaching in to offer her his hand but El refused to take it and burrowed in closer to Brogan.

"Get them all away."

Brogan's voice rumbled in his chest against her cheek and rang in her ears. Feet scuffed on concrete as Quinn and Steve did their best to make a clear path through the sea of gawkers. And that's what they were, not one of them pretended to be doing anything but staring at her. A couple of burly men made their way through the throng, pushing people aside willy-nilly as they headed for the back of the truck and Marcus.

"Come on. It's okay, I won't let anyone hurt you." Brogan cradled her against his chest and sidled along the seat to the door.

She couldn't help flinching as he stepped from the cab, she knew she was safe in his arms but the men had chosen the same moment to lift Marcus from the truck bed, leaving them within two feet of each other.

"Get him locked up." Brogan's booming voice quieted the crowd, a hushed silence descending.

One of the men collared and leashed Marcus, pulling him

away through the crowd. El breathed easy but the small comfort was short-lived when the crowd surged forward and surrounded Brogan.

"Jesus, give him room would you?" Quinn formed a barricade in front of them as Brogan moved forward.

People fell in step behind them as they made their way to the building and the door Steve held open. Questions flew around them but no one uttered a word until they were safely inside with the door closed.

"Steve, go over to the sheriff's office and tell William what happened."

"Shouldn't you do that?" Quinn asked.

"Later. First I want to make sure El's all right."

El leaned back and looked up at Brogan. "I'm okay, go do what you have to."

"No. Not until Doc checks you out and says you're fine. Plus I want to see Rowan before I leave the clinic."

"Quinn?" Rowan could be heard yelling from down the hall.

"Rowan's here?" El watched Quinn head across the room at a run.

"Yep, let me take you to say hi and then Doc can get a good look at you before I take you home." Brogan walked toward the hall on the other side of the waiting room.

"She's really okay?" The thought of Marcus hurting Rowan sent fear and guilt rolling in El's stomach.

"She'll be fine with a little rest and a few days to heal." A woman in a white coat met them in the hallway. "Take her into the room next to Rowan's, Brogan."

"Can she see Rowan first, Doc?"

"Let's leave that until after I get a look at her. Besides, I think Quinn will want to spend time alone with Rowan first."

Brogan followed the doctor into an exam room that looked

anything but sterile. The walls were painted with murals of animals and colorful mobiles hung from the ceiling. A closer look revealed all the animals were coyotes, young cubs at various stages of development prancing around the walls and leaping from the roof. Obviously this was the room they used for children.

"Sorry about the room but Rowan's in one and the other is full of supplies that arrived earlier today that I didn't get a chance to put away because of the emergency." She went straight to the sink in the corner, scrubbed her hands and pulled on a pair of latex gloves. "You can put her on the bed, Brogan."

"Right."

Brogan gently placed El on the exam table, making sure the blanket stayed wrapped around her. Not much point when the doctor would want to remove it to check her over. The discomfort swirling in El's stomach had nothing to do with her nudity beneath the blanket and everything to do with the events of the last few hours. Having Brogan at her side helped keep her from freaking out.

"Brogan you need to move so I can get at my patient."

Muttering what sounded like sorry, he stepped to the side, closer to El's head. He wove his fingers through her hair, brushing it away from her face, the soothing motion enough to distract her from what the doctor was doing until she touched a particularly raw spot on her ankle.

"Ouch."

"Sorry, this section has no skin left at all. I'm afraid it's going to hurt a bit more when I clean the dirt from your wounds."

El ground her teeth through the rest of the exam. While her ankles and wrists hurt she'd escaped any further injuries. The doctor still wanted to do a scan of her head to be sure she hadn't suffered any head trauma while unconscious but all signs pointed to nothing more than the minor abrasions on her arms and legs.

"I'm going to do a couple more tests, check your blood and get that scan organized but it won't be too much longer and you can go home." The doctor opened a cupboard and pulled out a bundle of cloth. "Here, you might be more comfortable in a gown."

"Thanks, Doc." Brogan helped her sit up and slip into the stiff garment.

"You're welcome." The doctor removed her gloves and held out a hand to El. "And it's a pleasure to meet you. Rowan's told me a lot about you, although I wish it were under different circumstances."

"Thank you, Doctor." El shook the offered hand.

"Please, call me Doc or Gordie."

"I'm Eloise but everyone calls me El."

"Okay, let me get you out of here." With a smile Gordie left the room.

She returned a few minutes later with a tray of implements El didn't like the look of. Seeing the vials to hold blood made her stomach roll and she quickly turned away to examine the mural opposite her.

Brogan held her hand while Gordie inserted the needle to take her blood for the tests. At the prick of pain El turned. The sight of her blood filling the plastic tube undid her. Light-headed, she swayed and if Brogan hadn't been next to her she would have toppled from the bed to the floor. Again. She was getting tired of playing the swooning female. Never in her life had she fainted but she seemed to be passing out at regular intervals since coming to Whispering Springs.

14

BROGAN KNEW he needed to go and face the Council about Marcus but he couldn't bring himself to leave the woman sleeping on the bed. He wanted nothing more than to take her home and forget the last few hours ever happened.

Rowan and Quinn quietly slipped into the room.

"How is she?" Rowan whispered.

"She'll be fine physically, not sure about her mental state though, the last few hours, hell the last couple of days have been rough." Brogan stood and pulled Rowan into a hug. "How about you? Baby doing okay?"

"I'm fine, we're fine. Twelve stitches in my head and a little sore but I'll live." Rowan pulled from Brogan's embrace and stepped up to the bed. "She looks exhausted."

"Yeah. I'm just waiting for Doc to give the all clear and then I'm getting her out of here." Brogan turned to Quinn. "You ready to face Council?"

"Whenever you are."

"Rowan, can you sit with El until we get back? I won't be long but if I don't show my face now they'll come looking for me and once I get El out of here I want no one and nothing disturbing her."

"Sure, you and Quinn go and get things sorted out because we all know William will be on our doorstep if you don't." Rowan settled in the chair Brogan had vacated.

"We'll be as quick as we can. Hopefully El won't wake until I get back."

"I'll be here if she does."

Brogan leaned over and kissed El's forehead. She didn't stir. Vowing to get back before she woke, he turned and headed for the door leaving Quinn to follow.

They found William and the rest of the Council members at the sheriff's office. The crowd on the street had dispersed to a degree but there were still more people than a normal day in downtown Whispering Springs. Brogan ignored all but his target, he didn't want this to take longer than necessary and if he allowed himself to be waylaid by a pack member it would be like issuing an open invitation.

"William, Councilmen." He nodded at the others briefly before turning back to the older man.

"Brogan, Quinn. Shall we take this indoors?" William's voice vibrated with tension.

Quinn was ahead of them, he stood with the door to the sheriff's department held open, waiting. Brogan ushered the councilmen in ahead of him. Dale Turner, the town's newly elected sheriff, met them in the foyer. Brogan had been glad when Dale returned to the mountains to take up a position with the local law enforcement a year ago. He was especially thrilled when the community had elected him to the position of sheriff six months later.

"Brogan, I've cleared the conference room for you." The sheriff extended his hand toward Brogan.

He shook the other man's hand. "Marcus?"

"Holding cell downstairs."

"Good." Brogan turned to the others. "Let's get this meeting done, shall we gentlemen?"

As at the front door, he allowed the older men to precede him. Each one gave him a wide berth as they passed. Brogan wouldn't hold it against them or bring up the fact they'd refused to listen to him or anyone else before now where Marcus was concerned. All he wanted was for them to declare him exiled and be done with it. He waited for them all to take a seat around the large table before closing the door and leaning against it.

One could hear a pin drop, no one spoke and each member of the Council found something other than him to look at.

"Do it." Brogan directed his words at William.

With a sigh the old man got to his feet, the legs of his chair scraping on the linoleum flooring.

"I, William Brant, declare Marcus Connelly exiled from Whispering Mountains pack and the area in which we reside. All in favor raise your hand."

One by one, the members' hands came up.

"Done." On a sigh, William sagged back into his chair, weariness etched in every line on his face.

"Sheriff, see that Marcus is escorted to his house. I want him guarded until he packs up and leaves. Anything else, William?"

"No, Sovereign. I expect to be kept up to date on Marcus until he's gone." Exhaustion laced the councilman's words and Brogan was struck but how old William was.

"I'll keep you both informed of all movements," Dale said.

"Good." Brogan pushed off the door. "Now if you'll excuse me, gentlemen, I have a mate that needs my attention." He opened the door and strode from the room.

Quinn followed a few minutes later. He and the sheriff

were deep in discussion as they made their way over to where Brogan waited in the foyer.

"Dale's going to personally oversee Marcus' departure," Quinn said.

"Thank you. I know we still have a couple of issues with one or two of your deputies and their continued support of the Connellys. I know I can trust you to see this through correctly."

"My pleasure, Brogan. It may have taken a while but we finally have just cause to exile Marcus. I'll make sure it's done."

Brogan reached over to shake hands. "I know I've said it before but I'm glad you returned home. You're just what the pack needs to continue on our path to a brighter future."

"Somehow I think that's more you than me but thanks for your praise. I'll be in touch later." Dale turned and headed to the back of the station.

Brogan and Quinn left the building in silence. He figured Quinn's mind was exactly where his was. On his mate. The sidewalk appeared to be empty but Brogan could see the pack members looking through shop windows, waiting in their cars and in small groups all looking in their direction. The whole town seemed to hold its breath as they made their way back to the clinic. He wouldn't be making any announcements himself but someone would have to tell them soon.

EL LIKED GORDIE. In the last thirty minutes she'd learned a lot from her. Waking to discover Brogan gone had frightened her but Rowan's presence had quickly put her mind at ease. When the doctor had joined them it was obvious the two women knew each other well and it wasn't long before the three of them were chatting like old friends.

She'd been shocked to find out Gordie had grown up here as a human, only being turned in her late teens. El didn't know the circumstances of Gordie's past but she did know she'd left the mountains for a few years before returning home to take over from her stepfather as the pack doctor. El planned to ask Rowan more questions later but she did manage to get several of her questions about the changes she was experiencing answered.

Gordie had also prescribed vitamins for the baby and strict instructions for complete bed rest until next week when she wanted to see both El and Rowan again. If anything showed up in the blood tests she'd give them a call, but that was unlikely. Rowan would need her stitches removed before then because of her coyote metabolism. The gash on Rowan's scalp would heal quickly and the doctor wanted to pull the sutures out before the skin attached to it and made it more difficult.

The phone rang in another room and Gordie excused herself to go answer it. El leaned back into the pillows and yawned. Fatigue stole through her and she closed her eyes. Rowan sat quietly in the chair next to the bed and El turned her head to look at her friend. Long lashes fanned out over pale cheeks and soft snores issued from between slightly parted lips. The day had taken its toll on both of them and she hoped Brogan and Quinn would return soon so they could all go home.

It was amazing how quickly she'd accepted Whispering Springs as home. The beautiful log house and the surrounding mountains had a history and warmth El felt to her very soul. She couldn't wait to go back and begin her life with Brogan. Smiling, she closed her eyes and snuggled into the pillows. Thoughts of a future with her mate filled with love and happiness eased her into sleep.

BROGAN STOPPED in the doorway to El's room, the sight of

the two sleeping women held him in place. El lay curled on her side facing Rowan, her back to him. Her tangled hair and the bruises and raw skin around her wrists and ankles a reminder of what she'd endured earlier. She'd proven her strength twice over in the last few hours. His anxiety over her size had all been for nothing, El would handle herself well when it came time to meet the pack.

His sister sat with her neck at an awkward angle in the armchair beside the bed, the white bandage around her head a stark reminder of the injury she'd sustained at the hands of Marcus. Anger stirred in his gut but he tamped it down. Knowing the man would never touch either of them again pleased him.

Breathing deeply, he stepped into the room. Three steps put him beside the bed where he pulled the blanket over El, covering the gape in the back of her hospital gown. He hoped not to wake her but she turned slumberous eyes in his direction. The smile that stretched her lips when she focused on him had his stomach flopping and his heart squeezing.

"Can we go home now?" Her sleep-slurred voice flowed over him. Her acceptance of his home as hers warmed him deep inside.

"Soon as Doc gives you the all clear." Brogan smoothed a hand down El's cheek and cupping her jaw, tilted her head so he could lower his mouth to hers. He brushed her lips lightly with his.

"Where's Quinn?"

He'd forgotten his sister sat next to the bed. Brogan looked over El to Rowan. "He's just finding Doc."

"She went to answer the phone." Rowan stood and stretched her back.

"Quinn will find her." Brogan straightened. "How are you both feeling?"

"Tired," El murmured.

"I feel like going home." Rowan sat back down. "Did you get everything sorted out?"

"Yes. The Council exiled Marcus and the sheriff is escorting him from the mountains as I speak."

"Good."

"Are we ready?" Quinn strode into the room followed by Doc.

"Ladies, it's been lovely chatting with you but I do believe it's time for you both to leave." Doc smiled at Brogan. "Did they exile him?"

"Yes."

She nodded before turning to El and Rowan. "I've given Quinn the bag with both your pregnancy vitamins and the cream for your abrasions, El. Rowan, I want to see you in a couple of days to remove your stitches and I'll see both of you in here in one week for a checkup."

Brogan helped El sit before scooping her up in his arms. Her arms slid around his neck and she snuggled in close to his chest. Warm breath fanned out over his neck and he placed a kiss on top of her head. He turned to find Rowan giving Quinn a stern look and pointing her finger at him.

"Don't even think about it, Quinn MacClellan."

Quinn raised his arms, paper bag hanging from one hand, and stepped back. "Didn't even cross my mind."

Rowan stared at him a few more seconds before walking from the room. Quinn chuckled and followed her through the door.

Brogan shook his head. He had no idea how Quinn was so in sync with his sister. She'd always been a complete mystery to him and nothing had changed in the months she'd been home. El squirmed in his arms, snapping his thoughts back to her and the need to take her home.

"See you in a week, Doc."

"If you're worried at all just give me a ring." Gordie followed him to the front door. "Here, let me get that for you."

Brogan stepped through the opened door to find his truck at the curb. Steve held the back door open and he slid El onto the seat before turning back to Steve and Doc.

"Thanks for everything today. I appreciate your help."

"I didn't do anything out of the normal, Brogan," Gordie said.

"No need for thanks. I've got your back whenever you need." Steve stepped back to stand next to Gordie.

"I'm still grateful for all you've both done." He climbed in beside El and closed the door.

Brogan pulled El into his lap. He stretched the seatbelt as far as it would go and snapped it in around both of them.

From the driver's seat Quinn asked, "Ready to go?"

"Yes." He squeezed El a little tighter. "Time to go home."

15

EL LISTENED to the steady thump of Brogan's heart beneath her cheek. Warmth radiated off him and flowed over her, soaking in to help shield her from the chill in the air. The drone of rubber rolling on tar, the murmur of Quinn and Rowan's voices and Brogan's words of reassurance that everything was okay, melded together in a soothing rhythm that comforted. Winding mountain roads swayed the truck in a rocking motion that lulled her to sleep as she lay in Brogan's arms.

Brogan held her close, stroked his hand up and down her back and dropped the occasional kiss on her head. When they pulled into the driveway it seemed like only five minutes since they'd left town, not an hour. Quinn parked as close to the house as the snow drifts would allow. The engine died and everyone moved quickly, cold air bursting into the cab of the truck as the doors opened.

El slid from Brogan's lap to the seat and waited for him to hop out. She climbed down, only to be lifted off her feet before they touched the ground. Holding on, she let Brogan carry her to the porch. Rowan opened the front door as they came up the stairs. A blast of hot air flew through the opening and surrounded them. The warmth smelled of spaghetti sauce and spices, everything that reminded her of home. El's tummy rumbled, the scent of her Grandma's special recipe sparking her hunger. Brogan laughed and continued into the house.

"Hungry, are we?"

"I guess so. I hadn't thought about it before now."

"Well, once I get you tucked up in bed I'll bring you some dinner."

"I can eat downstairs, Brogan."

"Nope. Doc said complete bed rest until she sees you again next week."

"I don't think she meant I couldn't get up to eat."

"Complete bed rest is complete bed rest, Eloise. That means no getting up for anything, including food."

They made it to the top of the stairs before El realized he was serious. "I think the idea was to take it easy but I'm sure I'm okay to get up for the essentials, like eating and bathing."

"There will be no getting out of bed for the next week. I want to make sure your body recovers from the traumas of the last two days." Anxiety and fear laced Brogan's words.

El sighed, she didn't want to upset him and if she was honest the thought of spending a week in bed with Brogan held an appeal all its own. He strode into the bedroom, kicked the door closed with his boot as he passed and placed her on her feet next to the bed.

"Do you need to use the bathroom before you get into bed?"

She shook her head.

"Okay, let's get you out of that ugly gown first."

He reached behind her to undo the ties of the horrible

green garment the Gordie had given her. The material wasn't the best, it was new and still held the stiff, rough feel all new clothes have before they've been washed several times. Once the ties were free, Brogan peeled the loose fabric from her shoulders and let it fall to the floor. Her nipples pebbled as the scratchy material brushed over them.

El shivered.

Being naked while Brogan was fully clothed sent an erotic jolt through her. After the day she'd had, sex should be the last thing on her mind but when it came to Brogan it seemed to be the only thing she thought about. He reached around her to yank the covers back before easing her onto the cool sheets. The idea of getting into bed alone held no appeal and El grabbed his hand to pull him in with her.

"Hey, none of that. You need to rest and if I get in there with you there'll be no resting anytime soon." He tugged to free his hand.

"I don't need rest right now, Brogan." She tightened her grip. "I need you to hold me. Need to know this is real and that we're both okay."

Brogan didn't say a word. He shook off her hold and began stripping out of his clothes. El scooted back in the bed and made room for him to climb under the covers with her. Warmth came off him in waves, banishing the chill in the bedding and the icy fear that had remained in her heart. They were safe, maybe not unhurt but safe from the man determined to do them harm.

El wrapped her arms around Brogan and pulled their bodies together until skin touched skin. Heat lashed out, zipping along nerve endings to set them alight with desire. Arousal swirled in the pit of her stomach, spreading out ribbons of warmth to drive her need for closeness higher. She smoothed her hands over his hot flesh until being held wasn't enough. She wanted to consume him—be consumed. Taken to the place where only Brogan could lead.

She covered his chest with open-mouthed kisses. Her tongue and lips teased each of his nipples until he moaned in pleasure. Sliding her hand between them, El circled his hard length with her fingers. The hot, pulsing flesh burned her skin and sent a shudder of delight into her core. With a firm grip, she worked her hand up and down his cock, smoothing her thumb through the bead of moisture that formed on the head.

"Jeez, El. You need to rest."

"No. I need this. I need to be as close to you as I can get." She stroked him harder.

"Christ."

Brogan's breath came in ragged puffs that blew at her hair and his hips jerked into her as he grew harder in her grasp.

"Dammit, El, we shouldn't do this," he ground out between clenched teeth as he grabbed her hand to stop her movements.

"Yes we should." El tilted her head back to look into his eyes. "Please."

He stared at her, the swirl of emotions in his eyes mesmerizing. Whatever he searched for he found, because in a heartbeat he pulled her hand free and rolled them until she lay pinned beneath him. Air rushed from her lungs, sucked out by the molten desire flashing in his gaze.

"Fine, but we do it my way, my pace."

Breathless, El nodded.

In slow motion he lowered his mouth to hers. The agonizing wait both excited and frustrated her. Brogan's tongue swept between her lips, delving inside to tangle with hers. She tried to take the kiss deeper but he pulled back.

"No." He spoke against her mouth. "My way."

His lips traveled across her cheek, butterfly kisses that soothed and seduced. Reaching her ear, he sucked the lobe into his mouth, nipped it with his teeth before his tongue traced the delicate shell. Warm air rushed over her skin leaving tingles in its wake. Brogan nudged her jaw with his cheek as he kissed his way down her neck and El turned her head to give him room to explore the sensitive flesh along her throat.

Brogan continued at his leisure. The unhurried pace tormented and teased El's senses until urgency filled her. Clawing at his back, she arched beneath him, tried to drag him closer.

"More."

"Soon." His hot breath bathed her nipple seconds before the tight bud was engulfed in wet heat.

El cried out. Pleasure rippled over her to center in her core. Her clit throbbed and moisture dripped from her pussy to coat her thighs. Brogan switched to her other nipple, one hand cupping her breast to lift it to his mouth. He sucked hard, drawing more of the tip between his lips. His tongue swirled around the tender peak and jolts of electricity fired off in all directions.

Her head thrashed on the pillow. The sensations bombarding her drove her closer to the orgasm threatening to crash over her. Brogan's hand left her breast, brushed over stomach muscles that quivered at his touch before sliding lower to cup her mound. Cream-slicked folds pulsed as he stroked her clit and El's hips bucked as the first wave of her climax gripped her.

A sob of desperation caught in her throat as Brogan removed his hand. He pushed a knee between her legs, shoved them wide and placed the head of his cock at her entrance.

"Not without me, El." He dropped to his elbows and cupped her face in his hands so she was forced to look at him. "Don't close your eyes. Watch me while I love you."

Through heavy eyelids, El focused on the emotions swimming in the golden glow of Brogan's gaze. Love, desire and need, with just a trace of fear swirled in a mesmerizing mix that she couldn't look away from even if she wanted to. He rocked his hips and entered her slowly. Her drenched sheath welcomed him, clasping his length as each inch pushed inside.

Buried to the hilt, Brogan held still. His gaze dropped to look between them and El raised her head to glance down at where their bodies joined. While they both watched, he pulled out. Her pussy walls clamped hard around him in an attempt to keep him from leaving. His erection, glistening with her cream, caused her muscles to flutter around the head, dragging a groan from Brogan and a shudder from her.

In long, drawn-out strokes, he made love to her. In and out. Push and pull. Brogan took them on a slow ride to the top. El wanted to feel his mouth on hers. Needed to taste him. Raking her fingers through his hair she urged his head toward hers. She captured his lips. Spice and warmth exploded across her tongue as they deepened the kiss. Urgency built—in the probing of his tongue and the thrusting of his cock—until their movements became frenzied with the need for more.

Brogan plunged into her body, strumming sensitized tissues and setting off El's orgasm. Wave after wave broke over her. His hips slammed forward, ramming his pulsing shaft to the hilt time and again. He sank his teeth into the side of her neck as he thrust deep one final time. With a guttural growl he came. Hot cum bathed her cervix, triggering a second climax. Her body bowed under him as breath stealing pleasure consumed her.

The rasp of harsh breathing filled her ears to compete with the pounding of her heart. Her nostrils were coated in the scent of sex and Brogan with every inhalation. His dead weight pressed her into the bed but El welcomed the burden. Their sweat-slicked skin grew tacky and cool as they came back to earth. He pushed up on his arms and withdrew from her body.

Muscles gone lax with satisfaction clutched at his retreating flesh.

Brogan dropped to the mattress beside her—one arm draped across her chest and sighed. His eyes remained closed and El reached over to brush the hair from his forehead. He murmured something unintelligible but didn't move. She smiled, had he fallen asleep?

"I love you." The words left her lips before she realized she was even thinking them.

"Love you, too." Brogan's usual deep rumble was muffled by his face being squashed against the bed. His eyes opened, the beautiful gold color full of the emotion they'd just spoken. "Come here."

Turning on his side, he pulled her close so they lay face to face. He dipped his head and kissed her, just a light peck on the lips. Leaning back, he studied her face for a few seconds. "We haven't talked about it but are you okay with being pregnant?"

She smiled. "More than okay. I can't explain it but everything just feels so right."

Brogan's hand slipped between them to rest over her still flat stomach. "I hope she's just like her mother."

El laughed. "And I hope *he's* just like his father."

"Maybe we'll both get our wish."

Her laughter stopped cold. *Two?* The thought of one terrified her in an exciting way, but two? She shook her head. "No thanks. One at a time will be just fine thank you."

Laughter rumbled in Brogan's chest.

"Are you still hungry? Want me to go get you some dinner?"

"No, I'm too tired to eat now, maybe later." She cuddled in close, tucking her head on his shoulder. "Just hold me until I go to sleep."

"I'll hold you longer than that, El. I'm not planning on letting you go ever again."

Her lips curved against his neck. He wasn't the only one who wasn't planning on letting go. She'd found the place she was supposed to be, the man she was meant to be with. There was no way in the world she was letting either go without a fight.

EPILOGUE

THE SUN SHONE bright and El couldn't wish for a better wedding day. After everything that had happened since she arrived in Whispering Springs, today was a welcome relief. Glancing in the mirror, she checked her appearance one more time. Pleased with what she saw, she took a deep breath and walked from the room.

Rowan met her at the top of the stairs, decked out in a beautiful wedding gown that was her mother's. Her best friend radiated with happiness. Getting to share this day with Rowan as more than a bridesmaid thrilled El just as much as the idea of being Mrs. Brogan Wilder in a few short minutes.

"Ready?"

"As I'll ever be."

"No second thoughts?" Rowan studied her carefully. "You've made some huge changes already, I'm sure Brogan would understand if you wanted to wait to get married."

"Are you kidding? That's probably the one thing I'm most sure of." El reached for Rowan's hand and tugging lightly she pulled her toward the first step. "Come on, our men are waiting."

Rowan laughed. "Yeah, and if we're more than a few seconds late they'll be charging up the stairs to come get us."

Together they took the steps a little quicker than normal, both excited to get the day underway. By the time they reached the bottom El knew this would be the best day of her life. Sharing it with her best friend added to the occasion but the best part was pledging her love to Brogan in front of the gorgeous mountains she now called home.

The yard was filled with people, most El had never seen before but Gordie met them at the door looking lovely in a pantsuit with snow boots.

"What can I say?" Gordie shrugged. "I'm a practical girl at heart."

El and Rowan both grabbed a handful of lacy white fabric and raised their skirts. Gordie looked down and burst out laughing.

"No one wants to deal with frostbitten toes on their wedding night," El said around her own laughter.

"I can think of plenty of other things to be dealing with that's for sure," Rowan added.

"Come on, everyone's waiting, two men in particular are getting a little impatient."

Over Gordie's shoulder El could see Brogan make his way through the crowd toward them with Quinn right on his heels.

"Speak of the devils," Rowan murmured.

As the men reached them a car pulled up the driveway. All talk stopped as everyone waited to see what the sheriff wanted.

Brogan slipped his arm around her shoulders and held her tight to his side as they waited for the new arrival to approach them. El didn't recognize the man who got out of the car but the vehicle and uniform told her he was head of the local law enforcement. When he smiled and offered his hand to Brogan she let out the breath she hadn't realized she was holding.

"Sovereign."

"Sheriff." Brogan reached over and shook the outstretched hand. "What brings you here today?"

"Thought you'd want to know Marcus Connelly drove his four-wheel drive off Stattler Bridge earlier this morning. We're working to retrieve the vehicle and the body now."

"He's dead? Are you sure?" Gordie asked.

"We believe so but we haven't found the body yet, it's not in the vehicle."

Brogan tensed next to her, Quinn stood straighter and Rowan sucked in a hash breath. Fear slid down El's spine. She didn't know why the three people closest to her would react in this way but when Gordie gasped and stumbled forward El knew Marcus driving off a bridge wasn't good news.

"He's not dead." Rowan turned to Quinn. "Until they find a body I won't believe he's dead."

"Sheriff, Rowan's right. Unless you recover his body we'll assume Marcus survived the crash. Which means the fight isn't over." Brogan squeezed El closer.

"We'll need to be on our guard until we know for sure." Quinn motioned Steve McKenna over. "Steve can you take Doc and the sheriff inside, we'll join you all in a minute."

"Quinn, I think we should go ahead with the wedding. Everyone will be leaving after the ceremony and we can deal with this then. We don't want people getting curious yet," Rowan said.

"I agree." Brogan said. "Are you all able to hang around for about thirty minutes? We don't have anything elaborate planned so it'll just be a matter of clearing everyone out of here."

"I'll need to get back to the search as quickly as possible but

I've left a good man in charge so I can give you one hour before I have to leave," the sheriff said.

"No problem, Brogan. Doc and I rode up together. We'll wait as long as you need." Steve moved to take Gordie's elbow but she avoided his touch by moving closer to Rowan.

"Okay, let's get you four married." Gordie pointed to Brogan and Quinn. "You two go to where you're supposed to be waiting patiently for your brides-to-be."

Both men did as they were told and headed for the pergola where the wedding was to take place.

"Let's get this show on the road." Rowan followed the men.

El feared what this latest news would mean but with Brogan by her side she was prepared to face any trouble that may come their way. She took a deep breath to calm her nerves and took the first step toward the man she'd come to love with all her heart.

BONUS EPILOGUE

FEBRUARY 14

BROGAN STARED through the frosty glass at the delicate flakes of snow drifting from the gloomy gray sky. The storm had been and gone leaving behind a snowfall that looked like glitter being tossed around inside a snow globe. Barely more than specks, each flake floated on the air going every which way as they descended to the ground.

So fragile yet so resilient.

Like his Eloise.

El slept in the big bed behind him; he should be snuggled beneath the warm blanket with her. Instead, he stood naked, gazing at the mountains behind his house. His mind was plagued with doubts and uncertainties but it was the guilt that had driven him from a warm bed before daybreak.

No matter how many times he ran recent events through his head he couldn't reason away the regret that continued to churn in his gut all these weeks later.

He'd listened to her time and time again tell him she was happy, that the decision to stay had been hers, except Brogan couldn't rid himself of the notion that his choices had robbed El of hers.

"Brogan?" Her sleep slurred voice drifted through the room, tickled over his skin.

He closed his eyes and savored the sound of his name on her tongue. That sexy accent he hoped she never lost flowed through his veins, settled low in his gut, and stirred heat in his groin, thickening his cock.

She'd said his name many times over the previous months and Brogan came to the conclusion that it was something he couldn't live without. No matter how much blame he heaped on his own shoulders.

"Mmm," he hummed without turning, waiting for the inevitable.

The covers rustled in the quiet of their room and he held his breath. "Come back to bed, Brogan."

Ah, there it was. Brogan recognized the tone of her voice—she knew what he was thinking about, knew he was likely beating himself up about something neither of them could change. It wasn't the first time they'd found themselves in this position.

El had been able to gauge his moods from the start but now they'd spent so much time together, he thought she might know him better than he knew himself.

"Playing it over and over in your mind won't change or help," she murmured, the covers rustling once more.

A sigh left his chest as his eyes opened. Snow still fell, a sparkling curtain of glittering white but the clouds had brightened some, the morning fast approaching. Winter might still have its icy grip on Whispering Springs but Mother Nature managed to show beauty in her cold brutality.

Spring was coming. Even now, green foliage poked out from under the colorless wet blanket that had covered everything around them for months, and the sun's rays kissed bare skin with warmth when the clouds parted long enough for it to show its bright yellow face.

As the sky lightened with dawn, a thin strip of blue licked the top of the mountains. Brogan smiled; the idea of seeing a clear sky later in the day pleased him. He had plans that didn't include freezing their asses off in a snowstorm. He'd barely gotten over finding El half frozen in one earlier in the season; he wasn't risking that again.

Turning, he leaned against the windowsill and folded his arms over his chest. El had rolled on her side and propped her head up on her hand. She studied him, her blue eyes taking in every naked inch of him—including the ones rapidly growing under her scrutiny. Brogan's chest tightened, the love and lust shining in her gaze pulling on the ribbons she'd wrapped around his heart.

She'd owned him from the moment his coyote had recognized her as his mate but since he'd gotten to know her, that ownership went deeper. He couldn't have picked a more perfect woman if he'd had a thousand years to search.

"We can say *what if* everyday but it doesn't matter. What is important is you and me. What we have is real and I refuse to allow you to question it any longer, Brogan."

He opened his mouth to protest but she cut him off before he made the smallest sound.

"No. I don't want to hear any more about choices taken away. I made the decision to stay, to be turned, and you know what?"

Brogan shook his head and pressed his lips together; she was on a roll, he didn't want to interrupt.

"I'd do it all again. Yesterday. Today. Tomorrow." She reached out the hand not under her head, leaned forward, and stretched it toward him, palm up. "Please, Brogan, put it aside and come back to bed."

How did he refuse a request like that?

El was his everything. Every thought, every breath, every beat of his heart, they all belonged to her.

His wife.

He still couldn't believe she'd married him days after meeting. But he couldn't deny the click, the rightness of them together. In spite of the guilt, he knew the fates had given him the perfect partner.

Pushing off the windowsill he made his way to the bed. "I love you," he said as he leaned over to brush his lips on hers. "I'll live with the any guilt if it means having you beside me for the rest of my life."

"Done." She threw the covers back and scooted toward the middle of the bed to make room for him. "Now get in here and let me warm you up."

He was rock hard now. The sight of El stretched out without a stitch of clothing on heated him up, it was a guarantee he'd be burning up once he climbed in beside her.

Smiling, he slid onto the bed and reached for her. "Come here; let's see how hot we can get."

EL HATED the regret Brogan felt over the circumstances that brought them together. In spite of the events that led to them mating, she knew she was where she was meant to be. With the person she was meant to be with.

He'd saved her. And not just from the storm that almost killed her when she'd first arrived in Whispering Springs.

He'd saved her from a lonely life and a bleak future. He gave her the bright, joyful future she'd once looked forward to but lost sight of when someone she'd trusted broke that trust and cut her self-confidence off at the knees.

She'd told Brogan all about Ken. How she'd realized she'd allowed him close because she'd been missing her best friend, Rowan.

It might have been Rowan's invitation to visit that had El boarding the plane all those months ago but it was the aching loneliness that had made the decision easy. And staying? Well, that was the easiest decision of all.

She got to live with her best friend again and who wouldn't be grateful to a friend who welcomed you with open arms and a hot brother.

Honesty made her admit it was the brother who had her staying. He might think he'd forced her decision, and he had, just not in the way he believed.

"I would have stayed regardless."

"What?" Brogan murmured as his lips brushed hers.

"If you hadn't marked me. I would have wanted to stay."

He pulled away, his gaze searching hers.

"I know you think you forced my hand but you didn't. I came here knowing things in my life were going to change. I was adrift in my old life. Rowan had left and then my business and confidence took a hit and I lost my way. Lost sight of what I'd been working toward. Hell, I'm not sure I hadn't already lost that long before Ken pulled the rug out from under me."

"I'd prefer it if you didn't mention another man while you're naked in my arms," Brogan growled.

"You can't be jealous."

"No. I have no need. You're mine and I know it. You know it. But the thought of how he treated you makes me want to hurt him. A lot."

"Ah, my hero." Smiling, she smacked her lips on his then said, "Is it bad that I like that you feel that way?"

"No. I'd expect you to feel the same if someone hurt me."

El frowned. "I wanted to kill Marcus."

"You almost did."

"Why did you stop me?" She'd never asked, he'd never explained, and she still regretted not taking Marcus out when she could have.

Brogan sighed. Brushed hair back behind her ear. "You were newly turned and while your coyote would have been comfortable with the kill, your human half wouldn't have been as easy with it."

"Yes, it would." She gripped his face in her hands, her gaze locked with his. "That man hurt Rowan, did terrible things to her long before the day he took me, but what makes me the most angry, the reason I'd rip his throat out if I could get my teeth into it, is that he hurt you by using me. That a coward's move."

"He saw you as a soft target."

"I'm not soft."

Brogan chuckled. "No. You've proven that more than once."

"You should have let me kill him."

"It doesn't matter now. He will never hurt either of us again. And again we seem to be talking about another man when you're naked in my arms." Brogan's hand slid down her side and around her waist. Pulling her closer, he said, "We've got better things to concern ourselves with right now."

Smiling, El wiggled closer. "Oh?"

"Hmm..." He lips brushed hers, once, twice. "Yeah, someone said something about warming me up."

"I did." Grinning she said, "What's the best way to do that, do you think?"

"Body heat." He slipped a knee between hers as he rolled them over until El lay beneath him. "Friction works best. You know"—his legs parted hers, his thighs spreading hers wide, his cock pressing into the open cradle of her sex—"rubbing bodies together generates the best heat."

El faked a shiver. "I'm really cold."

Smiling, Brogan rocked against her, his thick shaft sliding over her clit pulling a moan from each of them. "We should get as close as we can then."

She spread her legs further, bent her knees to open her pussy more. "How close?"

"This close." Tilting his hips, he thrust forward and entered her in one stroke.

With a gasp, El curled her spine, lifted her hips up, took him deeper. "Closer works."

"Closer always works."

"Enough talking. Get busy."

"Yes, ma'am."

As he withdrew, she locked her ankles behind his back and sank her fingers into the taut globes of his ass, tugging him forward. "Don't hold back. I want it all. I want all of you, Brogan. No more guilt, no more second guessing. I'm here because I want to be. Because you're it for me. You fit me in a way I've never felt before. A way I never want to live without."

"El..."

"I love you. Make love to me."

"I don't think I deserve you but I'm taking you anyway." He drove back in, ground his pelvis against her so his shaft pressed into her clit the way he'd discovered she liked. "You're mine," he gasped between thrusts as he picked up the pace.

"Yes. Take me."

Plunging deep he held still. "I love you."

Smiling, El gave his ass a squeeze. "Then love me."

"With pleasure." He started a push-pull rhythm that had

his cock touching every sensitive nerve in her sex, sending pulses of electricity deep in her core.

"Oh there's nothing but pleasure with you."

"*Us*. There's nothing but pleasure with *us*."

EL DREW IN A DEEP BREATH, relishing the cold filling her chest. The day had turned out sunny and warm. Well, warm compared to what it had been since she'd arrived. She still wore three layers, scarf, gloves, and a thick jacket.

"It's crazy how warm today feels."

Brogan chuckled. "The first sighting of the sun usually brings everyone out of hiding. If we went to town I'm sure the streets would be full of pack members venturing out for the first time in months."

"Is that normal? For everyone to hibernate through winter?" she asked, dodging around a rock on the path that wasn't really a path.

"Yes, and no. Some for sure, they lock down early winter and don't come out until after spring. Others like to get out between snow-ins."

"Should we go to town while the weather is good? You haven't been there for weeks and I'm sure you have sovereign responsibilities you should be taking care of." She hated the thought of him neglecting his people to spend time with her.

"No." He reached back to help her up a rocky section of slope. "If tomorrow's the same, and the prediction is it will be, then we'll go to town, have lunch at the Den, and I'll do whatever it is I might need to do and you can go shopping. I know Rowan keeps things well stocked but I'm sure there are some things we're running low on by now. We'll drag her and Quinn with us."

"Oh, I'd love to have lunch or at least chat with Doc, Tatum, and Kat. We haven't all been together since Doc's wedding."

"Whatever my lady wants," Brogan said with an exaggerated bow.

"Knock it off." She slapped his arm lightly. "Do we need to do anything for Wild Encounters? It's not long before you're up and running again."

"No. Everything is ready to go and having Brady on board means I can spend less time in the mountains and more time on expanding the business."

"You really think building a ski lodge lower down the mountain will be good? You're not worried about non-shifters finding their way up here?"

"Quinn and I have gone back and forth on this point for months. We've got safeguards in place. Plus they won't want or need to leave Whispering Slopes. You helped make sure of that with all your suggestions about shops and making the resort more like a town than just a hotel with ski fields."

"And you're staffing it with shifters only, right? Less chance of someone who shouldn't be directed up here being sent this way."

"We are."

"How long before you open doors do you think? Next winter?" She'd enjoyed being in on the discussions about expanding Wild Encounters and couldn't wait to see the company in action. Brogan had promised to take her on a couple of treks when he went out and she'd already thought about which of her cameras she wanted to take.

"No. We want to do this right, so we're not rushing things. The plan is winter after next and I'm not inclined to push that forward even if we are on track to do so."

"Oh," El gasped as she slipped on wet rock.

Brogan swung around and grabbed her arm, pulling her close against his chest and saving her from planting on her ass. "Whoa. Careful."

"Okay, this is getting harder and I haven't asked until now but where the hell are we going?"

"Not much longer. Up the top of this ridge is what we've come for."

Glancing up the slope, El decided she could make the next twenty feet or so. They'd been trekking for a half hour. Brogan had led her into the forest behind the house and urged her up the mountain. She wasn't against the trek, but after weeks of inactivity she was feeling every step of it.

Her thighs ached and her feet hurt where the new boots Brogan had bought her rubbed her heels and toes. It was a good thing it really wasn't that warm; without the slight numbing effect of the cold she was positive she'd be feeling it a lot worse.

"You go up first," Brogan directed as he moved her in front of him.

He kept his hands on her waist as they moved up the last of the slope and came over the top.

"Oh," El breathed. "It's... I don't have words."

The vista in front of them stretched for miles. Miles and miles of forest dusted in white. This was what people meant when they talked about a winter wonderland. It was magical.

"Dammit! Why didn't you let me bring a camera?" she asked as she spun around to face Brogan. If the view had taken her breath, the sight of Brogan sucked every molecule from her body. "What...?"

"Eloise, I know you come from a different world than mine and I wanted for us to truly combine our lives," he said from where he knelt at her feet. In his outstretched hand lay a ring. "Will you marry me?"

"Brogan." She sighed. "You didn't have to—"

"I know. I wanted to. So..." He lifted his hand higher. "Will you marry me?"

"I already wear your ring." She held up her left hand. "But my answer hasn't changed, won't change. Yes, I'll marry you every day for the rest of our lives if you want me to."

Slipping the beautiful sapphire ring on her finger beside her wedding band, he said, "The blue sapphire is for your eyes and the surrounding ring of smaller yellow sapphires are for mine."

"Brogan," she gasped. "It's gorgeous but what I love most is that you thought about this so deeply."

"I wanted you to wear a reminder of us together so whenever I'm not with you, all you have to do is look at this ring and know that I am in fact with you. Always."

Throwing her arms around his neck, she grabbed handfuls of his hair and pulled his lips to hers. Speaking against his mouth, she said, "You're already with me always. You live in my heart, Brogan. Forever."

Chapter 1

May Eighteenth

STEVE SAT ENCLOSED by darkness and listened to the sounds of the forest as it settled into the coming night. The sun had gone down hours ago thanks to the mountains he called home, but true sunset still had a few minutes. He'd lived in Whispering Springs or the surrounding mountain range his whole life. Never once had he felt the urge to leave it behind and explore the world. He took the occasional trip down the mountainside to visit one of the big cities, but there was no appeal in staying away longer than a day or two, a week at most.

He breathed deep, pulling the chilled, late-spring air into his lungs, the accompanying sting of cold meeting warm, a welcome twinge. His house had been finished for two months, but he hadn't moved everything in until this past weekend. A grin curled his lips as he thought about why it had taken so long. Having his two best friends somewhat occupied with Rowan's return had slowed down both the finishing of the house and the moving in. Not that he'd complain. Steve was more than happy Rowan had finally come home and even happier to see her reunited with her mate, Quinn.

The night around him grew still, quiet in a way that pricked his instincts, caused his hair to stand on end, and drew his coyote's attention. Steve slowly sat forward, leaned over to put his beer bottle on the deck beside his chair, before closing his eyes and honing his senses to listen—to smell. The crush of undergrowth beneath running feet hit him first, followed by a body-slamming gust of fear. He scented two shifters but he couldn't place them. Tried harder to separate them and connect either essence to the memory of its owner.

A howl of agony echoed up the ridge, sliced into his gut and pulled his coyote out with amazing speed. On his feet, Steve was glad he'd forgone shirt and shoes after his shower as he removed his sweats. Free of the restrictive garment, he shifted as he leapt over the deck railing to the ground one story below. He landed with a jolt to every bone but ignored it as he ran through the forest in the direction of the horrific screams of distress.

As he drew closer he could hear the struggles, smell the fear—the blood. *The enjoyment.* The attacker, in coyote form if he wasn't mistaken, was thrilled with his catch. A catch Steve had every intention of setting free. His muscles shuddered and it wasn't just from the exertion of running all out. He thought about stealth but a bloodcurdling cry and bark of triumph changed his mind. Low branches and shrubs slapped into him, tangled with his fur, as he powered his bulk toward the fight up ahead he glimpsed through the trees.

The other animal's head whipped up, yellow eyes and white teeth glowed in the dusk as he turned in Steve's direction. A frustrated howl rent the air as the coyote turned from his prey and bolted in the opposite direction. Torn between going after the retreating coyote and tending to the victim, Steve hesitated enough to have the decision made for him. Whoever the coyote was, he had too much head start and the metallic stench of blood told Steve his first concern should be the wounded human crumpled on the ground.

Ripped, blood-splattered clothes covered the too-still body, but there was no mistaking the feminine shape or perfume. He reached her side and shifted back to human form. Uncaring of his naked state, he knelt beside her head and felt for a pulse. The steady beat reassured him but how long would it stay that way? The overpowering aroma of spilled blood masked her scent, but he knew she was one of the pack, her scent was familiar. Too familiar.

No!

His fingers trembled as he brushed away hair to reveal the face he saw in his dreams and Steve's heart stopped.

"Doc?" The hoarse whisper ached in his throat.

His heart kicked back in with a thud. Adrenaline pumped through his veins and the urge to cradle her in his arms took hold but Steve knew he couldn't. Not yet. He had to check her injuries, stop the bleeding if he could. He ran his hands down her limbs to check for broken bones. In his limited knowledge he held back a howl of frustration. She was the one who should be doing this. She was the doctor. The person who stitched the cuts, set the broken bones and soothed the bruises.

Hands and fingers sticky with blood, Steve rolled her to her back and breathed a sigh of relief when she moaned.

"Doc? Can you hear me?"

She shuddered under his touch but didn't answer as he tried to find where she bled from the most. Her jeans and shirt were wet with blood but he couldn't find anything too deep or gushing enough to take the time to stop the flow. He needed to get her to the house. There he could remove what was left of her clothes and see how bad the damage was under light. He could also clean her up and decide if she required medical attention better than he could give.

They were about three hundred feet below his house but with the slope and thick vegetation, that distance may as well be three miles. It would take him longer to get up the hill than it had coming down with the burden of carrying Doc, and Steve knew every second counted. He tried to be as gentle as possible, but she whimpered when he worked his arms under her and pulled her against his naked chest.

In all the fantasies he'd had of Doc cradled against his naked body, this wasn't one of them. The woman set his blood on fire but carrying her now froze that same blood in his veins. Knowing someone had set out to hurt her—*had hurt her*—made Steve's coyote want to hunt down her attacker and do some hurting of his own. He turned and headed for home, careful not to let any branches scrape against her battered body. By the time he reached halfway, shivers raked her from head to toe and he knew shock had set in.

He lengthened his stride. The urgency to get her home giving him the strength to move over the ground quickly. When the large, dark shadow of his house came into view he breathed a sigh of relief and went toward the basement door. Once inside, Steve did something he'd never done before.

He closed the solid timber panel and threw the deadbolt home.

http://www.rhiancahill.com/books/coyote-hunger/coyote-whispers/

ABOUT THE AUTHOR

Rhian Cahill is the alter ego of a former stay-at-home mother of four. With motherly duties rapidly dwindling Rhian is able to make use of the fertile imagination she used to keep herself sane for all those years of slavery. Having spent years living overseas and visiting tropical climates has helped inspire some steamy stories.

Multi-published in erotic romance and contemporary romance, Rhian, with the help of Mr. Muse, spends her days and nights writing.

When not glued to the keyboard you'll find her book or knitting in hand avoiding any and all housework as much as possible.

For more on Rhian –

Website – http://www.rhiancahill.com/
Newsletter signup – http://www.rhiancahill.com/contact/newsletter/
Twitter – https://twitter.com/RhianCahill
FaceBook – https://www.facebook.com/RhianCahillAuthor
Instagram – http://instagram.com/rhiancahill/
BookBub – https://www.bookbub.com/authors/rhian-cahill
Goodreads page - https://www.goodreads.com/rhian_cahill

LOOK FOR THESE TITLES BY RHIAN CAHILL

Coyote Hunger Series

Coyote Home – Book 1

Coyote Wild – Book 2

Coyote Whispers – Book 3

Coyote Law – Book 3.5

Coyote Lies – Book 4

Party Games Series

Truth Or Dare

Spin The Bottle

Pass The Parcel – Novella

Are You Game Series

7 Minutes In Heaven – Book 1

Catch'n'Kiss – Book 2

Red Light, Green Light – Book 3

Hearts Are Wild Series

No More Talking (novella)

Dare You To (novella)

Mad Love

For a full list of Rhian's available books visit her website

http://www.rhiancahill.com/books/